BOURBON STREET SHORTS

SIX SHORT STORIES FROM THE JADE CALHOUN WORLD.

DEANNA CHASE

Copyright © 2014, 2015, 2016 by Deanna Chase

Cover Art by Ravven

ISBN: 978-1-953422-76-7

This book is a work of fiction. Names, characters, places, and incidents are products of the author's imagination or are used fictitiously. Any resemblance to actual events, locals, business establishments, or persons, living or dead, are entirely coincidental.

Bayou Moon Press, LLC

ENGAGED OFF BOURBON STREET

It's Christmas time, and newly engaged Jade Calhoun and her fiancé Kane are having a party at Summer House in Cypress Settlement. The tree is decorated, the mistletoe is in place, and the crab puffs are to die for. Nothing can spoil this celebration...except for some wayward magic and a pesky ghost who crashes the party.

CHAPTER 1

"Forget the cheesecake!" I yelled, clutching the flimsy limbs of the noble fir. I grimaced, unable to believe those words had actually flown out of my mouth. *Not the cheesecake.* But when a girl is suspended twenty feet in the air, on top of a wobbly ladder, she tends to get a little snappish.

Kane strode in from the kitchen, a pink ruffled apron strapped over his white button-down shirt and steel-gray dress pants. He waved a pink oven mitt that matched the apron. "What's wrong?"

I choked out a bubble of laughter, making the ladder shift again. "Shit!" Adrenaline shot through my veins as I clung to our enormous Christmas tree, praying I didn't end up splattered on the gleaming hardwood floor.

Kane ran toward me. With a flick of his wrist, the pink mitt flew over his shoulder. "Jesus, Jade." He grabbed hold of the metal A-frame. "Get down from there before you break your neck."

I shot him my best death glare. I was only up there because he'd ignored my last three requests to finish decorating the top three feet of the tree. But the worry clouding his expression melted my irritation, and I slowly moved one foot after the other down the steps, careful to not trip on the hem of my ankle-length skirt. "Someone had to finish decorating this thing. The guests will be here in an hour."

His strong arms came around me, lifting me off before I reached the bottom rung. "Forget the tree," he said in a low husky voice. "It won't be much of an engagement party if my fiancée is splattered on the hardwood."

A lock of dark hair fell over his gorgeous chocolate-brown eyes as he brushed his lips over mine. I closed my eyes, sinking into the kiss, his warm tongue sending electric shocks right down to my toes.

Yeah. Forget the tree. Kissing was much more fun. Good thing I'd remembered the mistletoe. If we positioned ourselves just right, we could go on like this all night. Except...

"Crap!" I yelped and pulled away. "The mistletoe! I forgot to hang it."

Kane's lips quirked. "I think we're doing fine without it."

"Let me down." Laughing, I pumped a light fist on his shoulder. "I promised Pyper. She has a plan."

"Huh?" Kane set me down on my feet. "What plan?"

"It has to do with Ian." I ran toward the grand spiral staircase. "I'll have to fill you in later." Dammit. I'd totally forgotten. If I didn't get the five bundles of mistletoe up in the next half hour, Pyper, my boss and Kane's best friend, was going to kill me. It was all she'd talked about for the last week.

I skidded to a stop at the top of the stairs and peered down the hall. Now, which room had I left them in? The office? Or the library? Maybe the guest room? We were having our combined engagement-holiday party at Summer House, Kane's family plantation house located in a tiny bayou town south of New Orleans. I was still settling in. This place was a far cry from my one-room apartment above Kane's strip club on Bourbon Street.

Hmm. The mistletoe had to be in the guest room. The one decorated in lilac. That was where I'd dropped my latest round of holiday purchases. And also where I'd been doing all my Christmas wrapping. I opened the door and peeked in. *Yikes.* Just what I thought. Chaos. Okay, it had to be in there somewhere. I trudged through the remnants of leftover wrapping paper and discarded shopping bags, scanning the mess. We'd only been there three days. I wasn't that much of a slob, was I?

After frantically searching each bag, I flopped into an upholstered chair and let out a huge sigh. Where was it? The wall clock read five thirty-five. Everyone would start arriving in twenty-five minutes. Time for a finding spell.

I closed my eyes and took a deep breath, settling my nerves. Working magic while in a frenzy rarely went well. But as far as incantations went, this one was pretty mild. I opened my eyes and stared at the white pillar candle resting on the dressing table.

"Ignite," I whispered.

The candlelight flickered to life. Perfect. I moved forward, but just as I reached for the pillar, the flame grew twice as large then split from the wick in four tiny orbs of fire.

"What the—"

The orbs shot around the room, circling me. I froze. A second later, they each zoomed to opposite corners of the room, lighting four other white pillar candles. The overhead light went out, and all five candles glowed brightly in the dark room.

Wow. That was…crazy. All I'd done was light a candle. Not all five. Maybe my power was still haywire after the soul-splitting thing two weeks ago. I didn't feel any different, though. Well, except for losing my empath ability. I hadn't felt one outside emotion in days. It was freeing but also weird, as if I'd lost a part of myself.

I shrugged off the nagging feeling that something had gone wrong. All I'd done was light a few candles. No harm, really. Twenty-two more minutes until the guests arrived. This time when I reached for the candle, nothing out of the ordinary happened. Thank goodness.

Holding out my arm, I closed my eyes and chanted, "Lost. Found. Lost. Found. Open my sight. Let the lost be found." Forming a picture of the five ribbon-wrapped bundles of mistletoe in my mind, I commanded, "Reveal yourself!"

The rustling sound of craft paper filled the room. I opened my eyes. To my right, a white paper bag shimmered with light. I smiled. There they were. "Come to me." One by one, the pretty little bundles flew out of their bag and landed on the bed in front of me.

Perfect. I scooped them up, blew out the candles, and ran back down the stairs. "Kane," I cried. "I need help." No way was I going back up on that death-trap ladder.

"I've kind of got my hands full," he yelled from the kitchen.

The delicious scent of roasted turkey permeated the air. Damn, that man was just about perfect. Gorgeous, rich, exceptional talents in the bedroom, and he cooked. I'd bet he even managed to save my cheesecake.

"Never mind." I didn't need a ladder anyway. I was a witch, after all. Eighteen minutes. No time to mess around. Five bundles. Okay. I placed one on the floor in our foyer, one at the base of the staircase, another under the chandelier in the ballroom, and one in front of the coat closet. And the last bundle was to go in the kitchen over the sink. It was a tradition of my mother's, one I was all too happy to honor. I set the last one on the dining room table and focused on the first four.

Instantly, they started to glow with sparkles of light. I raised my hands, and the bundles rose high in the air.

"Unite," I demanded.

Nothing appeared to happen, but when I lowered my arms, all four bundles were suspended exactly where they should be. That was easy. Except they still twinkled with light. *Huh.* At least they were festive.

I turned to grab the fifth bundle. "Kane?"

"Still busy."

I slid through the open door and leaned against the frame, smiling as I watched Kane mixing something with the electric beaters. "Whipped cream?" I asked hopefully.

He cast me a mysterious look and said in a gruff voice, "Come here."

How could I resist that? I snuggled up next to him, eyeing the bowl of freshly whipped cream. "Is that for my cheesecake?"

"No." He leaned in, nuzzling my ear.

"Shortcake?"

"Nope." His tongue darted out, sending a shiver down my spine.

"Pie?" I breathed as his teeth scraped my neck.

He chuckled, his hot breath sending a jolt of anticipation

south of my belly button. One arm wrapped around me, dipping me back off my feet into his strong embrace. He scraped the side of the bowl and brought a finger full of fluffy cream to my lips.

I opened my mouth. Yummy goodness melted on my tongue, eliciting a deep moan from the back of my throat.

"This," he said, heat in his rich-chocolate eyes, "is for after everyone leaves."

Oh God. How fast could I get rid of everyone?

Ting. Ting. Ting.

"Damn it," I whispered.

Kane's mouth covered mine, his tongue dancing over mine.

Ting. Ting. Ting.

I gently pushed him back, more than a little breathless. "They're here."

"They can wait." He dipped his head once more and clutched me close to his body as he made my head spin with one more toe-curling kiss. Everything pulsed.

He pulled away with a satisfied smile. "We should have mistletoe year round."

I shook my head, laughing. "This one's not even up yet." I held out the bundle. "Will you hang it for me?"

"Sure, but you'll have to pay for it." He winked and placed the whipped cream in the fridge.

I moved closer, intending to settle my debt.

Ting. Ting.

Damn doorbell. "I'm coming," I shouted and ran to the entryway. Right before I reached the door, it swung open all on its own.

"Nice trick," Pyper said, sweeping into the house. She wore a skintight red velvet minidress. Silver faux fur lined the hem and her wrists. For once, her hair was all black, any traces of shocking hot pink gone. I'd never seen her hair all one color before.

"Wow. Sexy," I said.

"That was the plan." She grinned and leaned in to give me a hug, but at the last minute, she planted her lips on mine and gave me more than I'd bargained for.

"Whoa," I sputtered, pulling away. Holy crap, she'd just slipped me the tongue.

I nodded to Ian, her sort-of boyfriend. "Has she been dipping into the nog already?"

He stared at us, his eyes bright with surprise. Then he gave us his easy smile. "Wow, that was some greeting."

Pyper laughed but turned away, and I swear her face turned the color of her velvet dress.

"Pyper?" I stared after her as she strode across the ballroom.

She cleared her throat. "I'm going to say hi to Kane."

I turned to Ian. "That was weird."

He grinned and moved toward me. Just as he leaned in, he pointed at the mistletoe above my head.

I jumped out from under the dang thing, flashing him an apologetic smile. "I need to get something from the kitchen. Make yourself at home." The very last thing I needed was Ian, the guy I almost dated before Kane, kissing me. Besides, I'd seen enough lips in the last five minutes. I scooted into the kitchen and leaned against the inner wall.

"I don't know why. It just happened," Pyper said to Kane, distress ringing in her voice.

"What happened?" I moved to stand next to Kane. "Did Ian do something?"

"No...I..." Pyper turned pleading eyes on Kane.

He snorted.

"It's not funny!" She smacked him on the arm.

I placed a hand on my hip. "What's going on?"

Kane draped an arm over my shoulders and whispered, "She's embarrassed about what just happened."

I frowned, not sure what to say.

"The kiss," Kane prompted.

"Oh… well." I bit my lip. "I was a little surprised, but it's no big deal."

"You're engaged!" Pyper blurted. "To him." She waved at Kane, as if we weren't aware. "And you're not gay."

I laughed. "No. But I'm sure I'm not the first straight girl you've ever kissed."

"Definitely not," Kane confirmed, his eyes crinkled in amusement.

"You're not mad?" she asked both of us. "I mean, things aren't going to get weird, are they?"

Kane and I glanced at each other. Then we both shook our heads.

I shrugged. "It's just mistletoe."

She glanced up at the bundle overhead and stepped forward. Then she seemed to consciously stop herself. She spun around, and without looking back, she strode back out into the ballroom.

I took Kane's hand in mine. "You're really not upset?"

He shook his head, his eyebrows pinched in confusion. "I might have been a little concerned if she hadn't been so wigged about it. But she didn't seem herself at all."

"So if she'd brushed it off as nothing, you would've worried?"

He glanced down at me. "I trust you, but she did steal my college girlfriend. A guy doesn't really recover from that

kind of thing, no matter how entertaining the fantasies are."
The crinkles around his eyes reappeared as a grin spread
across his face.

I punched him on the shoulder. "Shut up."

He laughed and handed me a tray of goat-cheese-stuffed
mushrooms. "Take these. I'll be out in a second."

"Hurry," I called as I headed toward the kitchen door.

A few moments later, Kane appeared by my side, still in
his pink apron.

"What's up?" I asked.

"You told me to hurry." He took the tray from me and
placed it on a side table.

I scanned him from head to toe. "You really want to greet
our guests like that?"

He glanced down at himself. "Uh, no." Laughing, he
pulled off the apron. "We'll need to get something a little
more masculine."

"Obviously." Summer House had been left to Kane by his
grandmother, and until I came along, he'd never spent any
time here. Hence the girly kitchen gear.

"Come on." I grabbed his hand. "Maybe you can kiss Ian
to get back at Pyper."

"Uh…"

"Kidding! Jeez."

Kane and Ian weren't on the friendliest terms. They
didn't hate each other; they just weren't buds.

In the few minutes we'd been holed up in the kitchen,
most of our guests had arrived. Kat, Lucien, Charlie, and
Lailah were huddled in the center of the room. Pyper was
standing near the front windows with Ian, fidgeting.

I waved her over. "Stop it," I whispered. "Everything's

fine. Take Ian off to one of the mistletoe bundles and get it over with already."

"Now?"

I couldn't believe how unsure and nervous she looked. "Yes, now. It's not like you've never kissed him before."

She swallowed. "Yeah, but that was before that reporter chick came to town."

An old flame of Ian's had shown up a few months ago, and according to Pyper, Ian had been preoccupied ever since. His budding romance with Pyper had come to an abrupt stop.

"Is she here?" I asked. "Did Ian invite her?"

"No, but he would hardly bring another woman to your party."

I put my hands on her shoulders and stared her in the eye. "This is not the Pyper I know. Take charge. Let him know how you feel. March over there and give him a little bit of that tongue you laid on me about ten minutes ago."

A bark of laughter escaped her lips. "Now you sound like Charlie."

We both turned to check out the manager of Kane's club, Wicked. My speech did sound exactly like something she'd say. She caught my eye, and I nodded a greeting. "Go," I said to Pyper and crossed the room.

Kat spotted me before I made it and flung her arms around me. "Mistletoe," she cried and then planted a kiss right on my lips.

The others all lined up to mimic her enthusiasm. After they'd each laid their loudest lip-smackers on me, we all laughed.

"Didn't any of you bring a date?" I asked, noting the large concentration of estrogen in the room.

"I did." Kat raised her hand and took a sip of her margarita. She wore an elegant fitted silk dress and had her salon-dyed red hair swept up in a twist. "Sort of." She pointed to Lucien. "We came together."

I raised one curious eyebrow. Lucien was tall, blond, and my second in command in the New Orleans coven. Kat could do worse. Way worse. "Nice," I said. "What are you doing kissing me with him around? Go. Play doctor or something."

"You were warm-up." She winked and glided off to join Lucien.

Lucien waved, and I smiled, nodding in Kat's direction just to let him know I approved. Not that he needed my permission, but she was my best friend, and I was his boss. Sort of. Leader of his coven. Close enough.

"Charlie? You're stag?" I studied her, taking in her spiky red hair and heart-shaped face. Tonight, she wore black skinny jeans, ankle boots, and a cream off-the-shoulder sweater. Supermodel material, that one.

She waved toward the downstairs powder room. "She's freshening up."

Lailah shook her head, amused. "Wait until you see her."

"Cute?"

Charlie caught my eye and chuckled. "You'll see."

"Just promise you'll let this one down easy," I begged.

The last two women Charlie dated, she'd sent a breakup text. They'd both stormed the coffee shop looking for her. At the same time. It wasn't pretty.

"Yes, boss." She saluted me with two fingers and disappeared into the foyer.

I didn't bother to ask Lailah about a date. She'd just ended an on-again, off-again relationship with an angel who tried to steal my soul. It was a touchy subject. I slid my arm around her waist. "You'll stick with me tonight. Come on. Let's meet new people."

We moved toward a friend of Kane's standing near the back door, chatting with Pyper. Ian leaned against the far wall, arms crossed over his chest, eyes narrowed. What happened there? Last I saw Pyper, she was off to make a move on Ian. Did she chicken out?

"Pyper," I called. "Introduce your friend to Lailah." I took off toward Ian, intending to find out what had happened, but Lailah fell in step beside me. "What's up?"

"I'm sticking with you, remember?" She tossed her honey-blond hair over one shoulder.

I stopped. "I didn't mean literally."

"Oh." Her face fell.

I mentally kicked myself. "Sorry. I didn't... I mean..." *Oh, shit. I should butt out.* She'd find someone when she was ready. "Let's go. You can help Kane."

She brightened and followed me into the kitchen. I grabbed a tray of crab puffs and headed back to the party. Lailah stayed behind. On the way out, I passed Pyper and Kane's friend.

"We need to talk to Lailah," Pyper said, tugging her companion toward the kitchen door.

"She's helping Kane."

Pyper smirked. "No. She's hiding. We'll be right back." They disappeared through the door.

Across the room, Kat had Lucien pressed up against the wall, her face glued to his.

"Wow," I whispered.

"She follows orders well," a voice whispered in my ear.

I jumped, nearly dropping my crab puffs. Right next to

me was a faint outline of a tall, dark-haired woman. She wore a high-necked, pale-pink ball gown, circa 1890. Taking two steps back, I glanced around, wondering if anyone else could see her.

"Who are you?" I whispered back.

She let out a high giggle and floated off across the ballroom.

Holy crap. We had a ghost. I spun, looking for Kat, but she was still plastered against a very disheveled Lucien. *Jeez, get a room.* Pyper, Lailah, and Kane were in the kitchen. Charlie was in the foyer, appearing to be having an argument with her date. *Oh my god!* Was that Candy Rhines? The one who starred in the new hit supernatural drama on Showtime? Dang. She *was* gorgeous.

A few of Kane's friends huddled near the punch, but I barely knew them, and asking them about a random floating woman didn't seem like a good idea. I strode over to Ian, who was sulking against the wall.

"What's wrong?" I asked, not sure I wanted to say anything about the ghost to him, either. Ian was a ghost-hunter. If I told him, he'd have his EMF detector out in five seconds flat.

A muscle in his jaw twitched.

"Ian?"

He averted his pale green eyes and ran a hand through his short blond hair. "Pyper… she told me… ah, shit."

"Told you what?" Uh-oh, what had she said?

He swallowed. "She wants to get married."

"To you?" I blurted.

"Yes, to me. You don't have to sound so appalled." His lips formed a tight thin line.

"Sorry. I'm just… surprised." Yeah. Very surprised.

Married? They'd barely dated. "I hadn't ever thought of Pyper as the marrying type. I didn't mean that the way it came out. What did you say?"

He pushed himself off the wall. "What could I say? I told her I was flattered, but that I wasn't ready for that. Hell, we've only been on a handful of real dates."

That wasn't what I'd had in mind when I told her to tell him how she felt. Had she lost *her* mind? "Yikes."

"You can say that again." He took off, heading for the hallway.

A tinkling laugh rang in my ear, and the ghost appeared next to me.

I shivered, but I wasn't cold. "Damn it! Stop that."

She smiled and floated across the room again. Lailah burst from the kitchen, Pyper at her heels.

"But he's perfect," Pyper badgered. "Lailah, you have to go out with someone eventually."

Lailah stopped in her tracks and turned on Pyper. "Not tonight, I don't. The only thing I have to do is help Kane in the kitchen." She turned to me. "Right, Jade?"

"No. I mean, not exactly."

Female voices rose in the foyer as Candy and Charlie's fight heated up. Kat lifted her face off Lucien just long enough to tell them to keep it down.

Pyper started in on Lailah again. "Philip is gone. Kane is taken. Stop punishing yourself." She grabbed Lailah's hand and started tugging her toward Kane's other two friends, who were staring opened-mouthed at Kat all but undressing Lucien right there in the ballroom.

The ghost materialized, glee written all over her face. She spun around, as if twirling in delight.

"Stop it!" I shouted. "Everyone just stop. This is a party, not a free-for-all."

Kat froze and then slowly untangled herself from Lucien. She turned to me with wide, shocked eyes and mouthed, "Oh my god." Color rose high on her cheeks. Lucien cleared his throat and straightened his rumpled shirt.

The shouting in the foyer suddenly became one-sided as Charlie seemed to retreat from Candy.

But Candy advanced, her finger pointed. "You're a disgrace. I can't believe you. I'm not a fucking puppet you can string along, thinking I'll do anything just because you're a great lay!"

Pyper, standing next to me, let out a surprised laugh but covered it with a cough. "Sorry." Her gaze travelled to Ian, and she abruptly turned around and hurried into the kitchen. Ian stared after her, then set his shoulders and followed, the muscle in his jaw pulsing with determination.

"Babe," Charlie pleaded. "You misunderstood. I don't want to break up."

"That," Candy pushed Charlie, making her back up under the mistletoe, "is exactly what you stood here and said. I quote, 'Before this gets out of hand, I need to let you down easy.' Unquote."

"I meant…" Charlie turned to me, her eyebrows pinched.

I held up my hands. "Don't look at me. I was only joking when I said to let her down easy because of what happened before. I didn't know you were even thinking of breaking up."

"Damn it." Charlie banged a frustrated fist against her thigh. "I meant if we ever did break up. Not today." She held out her hand to Candy. "Babe?"

Candy stared at her as if she'd grown three heads, but then her expression softened as she took Charlie's hand.

"Kiss her," I whispered.

To my surprise, even though I was positive Charlie couldn't have heard me, she pulled Candy close and dipped her back into a breathtaking kiss. The kitchen door swung open. Lailah stomped out, Pyper and Kane running to catch up.

"Wait," Pyper called.

Lailah froze and stared at Pyper. A look of horror flashed over her face before her brow crinkled in confusion. "Please tell me I'm hallucinating. That whatever just happened was a dream."

Kane stepped up beside me. He wrapped his arm around my shoulders. "You're never going to believe what I just witnessed."

I leaned into him, exhausted by all the emotional turmoil, not to mention the blatant sexual energy running through the room. "In the kitchen? Did Pyper kiss *you* this time?" I teased.

His face broke into a wide grin. "No. Lailah."

"Lailah? What?"

He nodded at where Lailah and Pyper stood. "Like that."

Sure enough, right in front of us, Pyper had her arms around Lailah, and they were going at it like two randy teenagers.

"Stop hogging." Kat appeared from behind us and edged Kane out of the way. She planted another kiss on my lips before I could move.

"Kat!" I pushed her away.

Lucien stepped in. "Hey, I thought that was my job tonight," he joked.

"You had your turn." Kat moved toward Pyper and Lailah. She placed one hand on each of their backs and leaned in.

"What the hell!" I shouted. "What is wrong with all of you? This is an engagement party. Not a bath house."

Charlie had Candy pinned against the stairs, her tongue down the woman's throat. Lailah, Pyper, and Kat were all kissing each other in some alternate lesbian reality. Pyper was bi-sexual, but my other two friends weren't. None of them paid any attention to my outburst. Lucien, Ian, Kane, and his friends all stared with their mouths gaping.

"That's it. No more mistletoe." I raised my arms and focused on the illuminated bunches suspended around the room. "Ignite!"

Four tiny fireballs erupted from my fingers and flew high in the air. Each hovered under the bundles for a moment, then all at once, they erupted in mini infernos, turning the mistletoe to dust. My girlfriends didn't even seem to notice, not even when the small amount of ash started to rain down on them.

Lucien whistled. "That was a fine piece of magic, Jade."

I huffed. "Didn't seem to help."

The tinkling laughter sounded from behind me again. "This is too much," the ghost whispered in my ear. "Best party ever. Even better than when Kane's grandmother threw her tea at the society ladies for gossiping about the young widow who took a lover. Oh my, the looks on their uptight faces when they realized their favorite silks were beyond repair."

"Do you see her?" I asked Kane.

"Huh?" He couldn't seem to take his eyes off my friends going at it three feet from him.

I turned to the resident ghost-hunter. "Ian?"

He, at least, had the decency to acknowledge me. He walked over to stand beside me. "Yeah?" He kept glancing at Pyper, an unnatural scowl gracing his normally genial face.

The ghost spun around, giddy in her delight of the chaos.

"Do you see that ghost?" I asked Ian.

His expression cleared, and he suddenly snapped to attention, eyes alert. He glanced around. "Where?"

I sighed. "If you could see her, you'd have noticed her by now." She'd moved to twirling around the threesome and laughing like a loon.

"Stop it," I yelled at her. "You're making me crazy."

The two make-out sessions ended abruptly. Pyper, Kat, and Lailah all stepped backward, putting about ten feet between each other. Kat covered her mouth with her hand. Lailah stood frozen, not meeting anyone's eyes. Pyper glanced around in confusion, met Ian's eyes, and took a few more steps back.

"Jade?" Kane whispered. "Did you just spell them?"

"No." I would have noticed a little spark of magic if I'd had. *Right?* I wasn't so powerful that I could make things happen without even knowing about it.

Except... I had with the candles earlier.

Candy pulled Charlie toward the front door. "Let's go. I can think of better places we can... you know."

Charlie wrapped her arm around Candy's waist but shook her head, a small smile touching her lips. Candy started whispering in Charlie's ear, and although Charlie laughed, she didn't let Candy drag her out.

My other three friends were all avoiding each other's gazes.

"What was that?" I demanded.

All at the same time, they said, "You told me to kiss her."

"Huh?" What were they talking about? I'd mumbled for Charlie to kiss Candy, but not the rest of them.

"Hahahahaha. Oh, I do love the effect of mistletoe," the ghost sang as she floated near me. "It always makes for an interesting party."

"Is the mistletoe spelled?" I asked her. "Did you have anything to do with this?" Ghosts did carry energy, and if she'd been a witch in life, she could have altered them.

"Who are you talking to, Jade?" Kane asked.

"The ghost," I snapped, losing the last of my patience.

Beside me, Ian pulled his EMF detector out of his jacket pocket and flipped a switch. A red light lit up, indicating it was on.

I rolled my eyes and pushed him aside. Did he take that thing everywhere?

"Oh, wow," he said. "The reading is off the charts."

"Of course it is. She's right next to you." I shook a finger at her. "Tell me what's going on right now. Or I swear I'll let him exorcise you right out of this house."

She stopped her girlish twirling and peered at me. "He can't do that. In ninety years, no one has managed it." She smiled and started to glide over to the stairs.

"He's done it before. In fact, we all sent one to Hell last year. You could be next," I lied. While we could probably open another portal to Hell, I wouldn't risk it on a ghost who, while annoying, seemed relatively harmless.

That stopped her mid-float. Kane put his hand on my back in a show of support. The rest of my friends started to move closer together, though they showed no signs of making more sexual advances. Thank the gods.

Lailah took a spot next to me, her gaze trained on the ghost. She narrowed her eyes and said, "Reveal."

The ghost's eyes went round with shock as she shimmered and suddenly appeared almost solid. Everyone in the room gasped, and chatter erupted.

"Nice trick," I told Lailah, our resident angel. She had skills unlike anyone else's. "Did you not see her before?"

Lailah chewed on her lip and stared at her feet. "I wasn't paying attention."

"Oh." *Right.* I moved closer to the ghost. "Now spit it out. What's going on here?"

Ian stepped away from the crowd, his hands full of even more beeping electronics. He actually glowed with excitement. I couldn't stop the *Ghostbusters* theme song from running through my brain.

"You did it," the ghost blurted. "When you used those spelled candles from the lilac room to find the mistletoe."

"Spelled candles?" I asked.

"The pillars. They have magic. They've been here forever. This is only the third time a witch has lit them. Usually, the magic enhances the power of the witch, but since you used them to find the mistletoe, it made people want to kiss you. Then it gave you power over those who did."

She backed up, her arms crossed over her chest as she glared at Ian, a sneer on her lips.

"Oh, stop it," Pyper snapped. "He isn't going to do anything to you. He just likes data."

I would've been pissed at Pyper for spoiling our upper hand with the ghost, but a light bulb had popped up over my head with her explanation. All the weird behavior my friends participated in had been a direct result of something I'd told them to do. Pyper telling Ian how she felt. I mean, I had no idea she wanted to marry the guy. I'm certain she never would have said anything like that of her own free will. She kept her emotions pretty close to the vest.

Charlie had let Candy down easy, though she had no intention of breaking up with her. Kat attacking Lucien had been at my suggestion. Though I'd only said to kiss him, not have an almost X-rated adult show. Lailah stayed in the kitchen all night, helping Kane. Pyper tried to set Lailah up with Kane's friend. And finally, the kissing episode. I'd prompted all those things. I closed my eyes and took a deep breath.

"Guys?" I opened them to everyone staring at me. "This is all my fault. All the crazy stuff everyone did was something I'd said to do, only taken literally. Very literally and not at all in the way I intended."

I bit my tongue. So much for helpful advice. That would teach me to stay out of other people's business. No one said anything. They only stared expectantly at me as if I could erase their embarrassing behavior.

"How do I void the spell?" I asked the ghost.

She glided toward the stairway.

"Camille?" Kane said.

She stopped and eyed Kane with a look of wonder. "You know me?"

He shrugged. "I know of you. Come back over here until Jade is satisfied with your answers."

She pursed her lips and balled her fists, but she floated back.

He smiled. "Mamaw once told me she'd heard a rumor about a ghost bound here, and that she had to obey any direct orders from the owner. Looks like we're in luck."

Jesus. I loved how Kane took everything in stride. I beamed up at him. "You're amazing."

He kissed the top of my head. "You too, love."

I turned to Camille. "How do I free my friends from this spell?"

She glared.

"Answer her," Kane demanded.

By then, everyone had formed a circle around Camille, most of them awed by the ghost sighting. It was remarkable none of them had run screaming from the house. But my friends had been through a lot the last year. An 1890's ghost was probably pretty tame compared to demons and black magic.

Camille's shoulders sagged as if she'd lost a great battle. "Fine. Repeat after me."

I nodded.

"Candles of Summer House, release your hold. Bind your will to mine and rest for another season." She stared at me, her steel-gray eyes raging with defiance.

"Try again," I said quietly and released a thread of coven magic, just enough to form the five-point pentagram at Camille's feet but enough to let her know that *I* knew what that spell meant. I would not be bound to any foreign magic, and that was what a binding did.

Panic flashed in those gray eyes. "I mean...uh... sorry, it's been a long time. And I'm dead."

"Handy excuse," Pyper said, her trademark sarcasm firmly back in place.

Camille tried to back up, but the unintended circle held strong. "Okay. This should do it. Candles of Summer House, release your hold. Your magic is not welcome this night."

I met Lucien's gaze. He gave a slight nod. Yes, I thought that was safe enough. I repeated Camille's words and added, "Contain your power within your wick, for the leader of the

New Orleans coven shall control your magic from this day forward."

Camille gasped. "How dare you? That was my only access to power, and you just took it away from me! I'm dead. Don't you understand? It was all I had left." Her image flickered as she shot straight up in the air. "You'll pay for this, Jade Calhoun. Mark my words. You'll pay."

"Not tonight, Camille," Kane said, his voice calm. "Go away now. You've caused enough trouble."

Before she could open her mouth again, she vanished.

"No! Damn it." Ian waved his EMF detector in the air. "Those were some of my best readings ever."

Pyper burst out laughing. "Ian, dude, the ghost was right in front of you. Just enjoy that for now." She grabbed his hand and tugged. "We need to talk."

"Oh?" Ian was so far into his work, he'd obviously forgotten about the marriage revelation.

"Yeah, we need to clear up an earlier conversation." She gave me a reassuring smile and dragged a distracted Ian into the den.

"Jade, Kane?" Charlie called. "I'm going to take Candy home. We've got to… well, I'm sure you can figure it out." Her wicked smile left nothing to the imagination.

I laughed. "See you later."

Kane waved, and the door shut softly behind them. Kane's friends said hasty goodbyes, both appearing dumbstruck. That left Lucien, Kat, and Lailah. The three offered to help us clean up, but I shooed them away. All I wanted to do was eat cheesecake and go to bed, preferably both at the same time.

Lailah barely met Kat's eyes as she said goodbye and told me she'd call me later. Kat and Lucien stayed glued together.

They left shortly after. From the way they were looking at each other, it wasn't hard to guess what they'd be up to as soon as they got back in the French Quarter. Maybe the night wasn't a total disaster.

Ian and Pyper emerged from the den, joking about drive through Elvis chapels. When Kane questioned them about it, they doubled over laughing, barely able to breathe. Okay. Maybe someone really had dipped too much nog. They were holding hands and still laughing when they left. Hand holding was better than glaring. It was progress.

I grabbed a dirty tray and headed into the kitchen.

Kane joined me at the sink a few minutes later. "Not exactly the party we planned."

"Ha. No, not exactly." I started scrubbing melted cheese from the tray.

"It's one of the things I love about you." Kane took the tray from me and set it aside.

"What's that exactly? That I attract ghosts and demons? Or that my friends all seem to be closeted lesbians?"

He chuckled. "No. I love that every day is a surprise." His arms came around me, and he leaned in. He stopped just before our lips met. "Are you up for this?"

"Kissing you? Always."

"No, the consequences." He pointed up.

Above us was the fifth glowing mistletoe. Ah, I'd forgotten about it. If he kissed me right there, he'd have to do whatever I said.

A devilish smile made my lips twitch. My eyes met his eager ones. "Yeah," I breathed. "You?"

"Always." His warm, demanding lips met mine, nipping and teasing as our tongues danced together. Seconds later, I pulled back, breathless. "Ready for cheesecake?"

He nodded, heat in his eyes.

I pointed to the refrigerator. "You grab the cake. I'll get the utensils."

"Who needs utensils?" he asked, his gaze running the length of my body.

I laughed, a low sexy sound, and dropped the forks back in the drawer. I grabbed the whipped cream and moved to the door. "After you."

He glanced over his shoulder to watch me watching him. "As you wish, my pretty witch."

Oh. My. Cheesecake, whipped cream, and a submissive Kane. I licked my lips. Forget the party. The night had just begun.

SPIRITS OF BOURBON STREET

It's Halloween on Bourbon Street, and white witch Jade Calhoun is ready to party. But when a sexy spirit traps everyone in the past, she's forced to forgo the cocktails in order to save those she loves...again.

CHAPTER 1

"*H*oly abs," my best friend Kat whispered as she gawked at the half-naked male standing in front of Pyper. He was dressed only in beige linen pants and brown leather work boots. "Where did she find him?"

I laughed and hung our costumes on a rolling rack. We had converged in a meeting room just off the grand ballroom in the Jean Baptiste Hotel. In just five short hours, we'd be throwing the most exclusive Halloween party on Bourbon Street. And part of the entertainment was body-painted servers. "Probably the modeling agency. Or he could've answered the call on her website."

Kat fanned herself with her hand, her emotional energy giddy with attraction.

"Stop. You're entirely too into that guy, and it's making me uncomfortable." Kat was my best friend, and because I was an empath, I was pretty much always tuned in to what she was feeling. Usually that wasn't much of a problem, but when it came to sexual energy, it just made me feel gross. There were some things I shouldn't be privy to.

Kat ignored my remark and said, "He doesn't look like a model."

I had to agree with her. The ones that Pyper usually hired for her body-painting gigs were metrosexual in the extreme; bodies entirely waxed, hair styled with fruit-scented products, and often wearing concealer to hide any blemishes. They were pretty, but not manly men. Not like the perfect specimen standing before us.

He had a couple days' worth of growth in the facial hair department, thick, wavy, dark locks that fell to his chin, and a well-defined upper body without an ounce of extra weight. He had broad shoulders and a trim waist, his muscles well defined but not bulky. And judging by the slight farmer's tan, I guessed his workouts came in the form of construction rather than weightlifting. He was ruggedly handsome in the extreme.

"They don't make them like that anymore," Kat said.

I elbowed her and was treated with another wave of her barely suppressed lust. Closing my eyes, I imagined my glass silo, the one I used to block out other people's energy, and sighed in relief when I could no longer feel anything radiating from her. "You have a man. A gorgeous one."

She grinned at me. "Oh, I know. Believe me, I haven't forgotten. Did I tell you what he did to me last—"

"La, la, la, la, la," I chanted, sticking my fingers in my ears. "I told you I don't want to hear about any more sexcapades between you and Lucien. He's my second-in-command. I don't want to be picturing the two of you…doing whatever it is you do when I'm at the next coven meeting."

She shook her head, laughing. "God, Jade. How can you be such a prude when your husband owns a strip club?"

"One has nothing to do with the other. Besides, I'm not a prude. I just don't need the details."

"Whatever you say." She scooted closer to Pyper and asked, "Where's everyone else?"

The black-haired beauty finished outlining the design on her model's chest. "They'll be here in an hour or so. Julius was a little early, so we went ahead and got started. Check it out." Pyper waved me over and pointed to a jagged line she'd drawn on his chest. "See this?"

Kat and I both nodded.

"I'm going to paint a skeleton hand ripping his heart right out of his chest. What do you think?"

Kat grimaced. "It's awesome. And a little gruesome."

"Well it *is* a Halloween party," I added. "And it sounds amazing. Can't wait to see what everyone else is going to look like."

Pyper winked and went back to work on Julius. He was completely fixated on her every movement. I had a hard time deciding if he was enamored with her work or just her. She was tiny, with a dancer's body, and had black hair with a bright electric-blue streak in the front. She was sexy as hell and usually a total flirt. But at the moment, she was all business.

She glanced up at him. "Do you need a break?"

"From what?" he asked, his blue eyes nearly searing her with their intensity.

She stepped back and averted her gaze as she vigorously dabbed her dirty paintbrush over a clean surface of her painter's palette. Only instead of wiping off the excess, she pushed it through two colors, making an even bigger mess. "Oh, crap!" She tossed the brush into a cup of water and put everything down, wrinkling her nose. "From standing still. If you need to sit for a while, just let me know."

"No. I'm fine here." He pulled his shoulders back and seemed to grow an inch or two taller.

"Look at those shoulder muscles," Kat said, fanning herself again. "Whoa. I think I need a drink."

Pyper glanced back at us, her expression amused. "I think we could all use a cold one. Get us something from the bar?"

"Sure." I suppressed a laugh and yanked on Kat's arm, pulling her into the grand ballroom. "You need to cool off."

She frowned and shook her head as if trying to dislodge whatever had come over her. "Wow. I don't know what happened back there, but either I was spelled or my hormones took a turn down slutville alley."

I slipped behind the temporary bar and pulled a couple of beers from a giant bucket of ice. "Spelled? You think he was a witch of some sort? What did he do, cast a lust charm?"

"Oh, shut up," she said, smiling. "It could happen."

"Maybe. But I don't think so. I would've felt something." The thought had me frowning in confusion. I hadn't gotten a read on Julius at all, had I? When we'd first walked in, I'd felt Pyper's intense concentration and then Kat's inappropriate lust connection, but I hadn't sensed one thing from Julius. Interesting.

"Well, whatever it was, I'll stay here. If I'm gonna start in on that beer, I don't want to get caught drinking and drooling."

"Good plan." Chuckling, I opened two Abita Ambers and retreated back into the meeting room. "Okay, beers—whoa." I stopped in my tracks and gawked. Pyper was wrapped in Julius's arms, and the pair of them were going at it like sex-starved teenagers. He had one hand on her ass and the other curled into her hair, while she had one leg wrapped around his waist and her nails dug into his bare shoulders.

I silently placed the beers on the nearest table and backed up slowly, trying my damnedest to not be seen. I was almost to the door when—

"Oomph."

I ran smack into someone coming in from the other room. "Oh, no, I'm so sorry," I said, spinning around right into the arms of Kane, my husband. *My husband.* Was I ever going to get used to thinking of Kane that way? We'd been married for six months, and I still got giddy every time he called me his wife.

"Hey there." He circled his arms around me. "Where are you going in such a hurry?"

I grimaced and jerked my head toward the make-out twins.

Kane glanced over my shoulder and grinned. "Oh, I see." He inclined his head in greeting. "Hey, Pyper. Looks like we might be intruding."

"Uh…well, no, not exactly," I heard her say breathlessly.

Kane laughed while I turned around and sent her an apologetic look. She was completely rumpled, her face flushed, and her smock smudged with beige and white body paint.

"We'll be in the other room," I said and tugged Kane back into the ballroom as fast as I could.

"Well, that was interesting," Kane said, wrapping his arms around my waist.

"Interesting?" I glanced up at him, exasperated. "He's a client. And what about Ian? Holy cow. What if he'd walked in?"

"Oh my God! Is Pyper macking on that model?" Kat asked, her eyes alive with excitement.

Kane nodded, his lips curled into a ghost of a smile.

"Oh, good for her. Someone needed to taste that delicious piece of man meat."

I shook my head. "Does no one care about Ian? Did you two forget about him?"

"Ian's out of town. Again," Kat said. "He's working on that ghost-hunting cable show with what's-her-name. The high school friend that has a crush on him. If I had to guess, he's not exactly worried if Pyper walks in on him, if you know what I mean."

Kane grabbed a beer from behind the bar. "About time she moved on. Ian's been gone more than he's been home for the last three months."

"But that's work," I said. "Don't you think we need to give the guy the benefit of the doubt?"

"I would if he stayed in touch." Kane's expression turned flat with irritation. "Did you know she hasn't heard from him in over two weeks? Not even a text."

I frowned, worried now. Ian wasn't the typical guy. He was a ghost hunter and was known to care more about his work than anything else. But going a few weeks without touching base with Pyper wasn't normal, even for him. "Something must've gone wrong on his investigation. He'd never—"

"I talked to him yesterday." Kat popped a piece of chocolate in her mouth. "The investigation isn't leading to anything. He's considering going to another site before he comes home."

"Seriously?"

She nodded. "I think they might've already broken up, but neither is really talking about it."

The door flung open and Pyper came striding into the ballroom, wearing a fresh smock. She grabbed my arm and tugged me over to a corner away from Kane and Kat. "I need a favor."

"Like a reminder you have a boyfriend?" I asked as gently as possible.

"Oh, fuck Ian." She scowled. "He wants to break it off but doesn't have the balls to do it."

I raised my eyebrows. "And you know this because...?"

"He said as much the last time I talked to him. Something about needing some space and having to figure out what he really wants. You know, guy code for 'I don't want to be an ass.' Whatever, I'm over it. Forget him. I need you to be my chaperone for the rest of the day. I don't know what it is about Julius, but when I'm around him, I can barely control myself."

I cast a glance at Kat. "You're not the only one."

She followed my gaze. "She felt it too?"

"Yeah. But I didn't." I pursed my lips in thought. "It's weird. I didn't feel anything radiating off him."

"Good." She grabbed my hand and tugged me back toward her workroom. As we passed Kane, she said, "I'm borrowing your wife for the rest of the afternoon."

Kane bent and gave me a soft kiss. "Take care of her."

"Yeah. Sure. Whatever." Pyper pushed the door open and then stopped dead in her tracks.

I glanced around the deserted room, my heart sinking for her. In the short time she'd been in the ballroom, Julius had vanished.

CHAPTER 2

"*I*nteresting costume choice," Kat said, eyeing me.

I glanced down at my slutty red-leather demon outfit. The micro-mini showed ample leg, while the bodice did a fine job of amplifying my cleavage. "What? Cliché?"

"In the extreme. But fitting, I guess, considering you hang out with your fair share of demons and angels."

"Funny." I smirked. "And what are you supposed to be, a milkmaid?" I asked, eyeing her lace-up black-and-white bodice and poufy red skirt.

"Oh." She shrugged into a red hooded cape and twirled. "Little Red Riding Hood. Better?"

"Much." I secured a staff badge to my outfit and passed one to Kat. "Ready?"

"Yep."

Kat followed me out of the hotel's meeting room and across the hall to the ballroom. The party was scheduled to start in thirty minutes, and we just needed to do a quick sweep to be sure all the last-minute details were in place.

"Can you check with the girls at the raffle-ticket table and make sure they have everything they need?" I asked her.

"Sure. What's the prize?"

"VIP tickets and balcony access for Mardi Gras." The party was being thrown by one of Pyper's biggest clients. He was a music producer and often threw parties to promote his musicians. He'd employed Wicked, Kane's club, to see to all the details, even though the party was being held in the hotel. The club just wasn't big enough.

While Kat made sure the raffle was ready to go, Pyper, Charlie and I stuffed the gift bags of CDs, USBs, and other swag. Thirty minutes later, the booze was in place, the dancers were standing by, and all we needed was the partygoers.

"Hey, beautiful," Kane said, grabbing my waist from behind.

I twisted in his arms and let my gaze wander from head to toe. "Hey, yourself." I raised one eyebrow, taking in his kilt, the demon-hunter dagger strapped to his belt where a traditional dirk would be, and the white linen shirt that was partially open, revealing his chiseled chest. I resisted the urge to check my chin for drool. Holy eff, he was hot. "A highlander?"

He winked. "I thought you'd like it."

Suddenly I was very warm in my little leather dress. "'Like' might not be a strong enough word."

A seductive laugh rumbled from his throat as he leaned down and then whispered, "Maybe later, if you've proven yourself a naughty little devil, I'll let you see what's underneath."

I rolled my eyes to hide the fact I wanted to jump him right there. Goddess above, kilts should be illegal on a man as sexy as Kane Rouquette. "I'm never naughty," I said, batting my eyes innocently.

"Never?" He ran his fingers down my neck and lightly brushed them over the crest of my breast. A ripple of anticipation shuddered through me, and I shamelessly arched into his touch.

"Maybe not never," I breathed and tugged on his shirt, yanking him to me. And when I looked up into his desired-filled dark-chocolate eyes, I melted right there in the middle of the ballroom.

I wanted nothing more than to push him back into the meeting room, slide my hands up under that kilt, and have my way with him in every way possible. My gaze landed on his partially opened lips. "Kiss me," I demanded.

"Aye," he said in his fake Scottish accent. Then his lips were on mine, his teeth nipping at my bottom lip as he tightened his grip around me.

I was lost in his demanding kiss, pressed against his hard body, my head swimming with not only my own intense need, but his too. Every part of me was on fire, aching to be touched.

His hands landed on my hips, his fingers gripping me hard. "Jade?"

"Yeah?" I tilted my head slightly and took the lead, kissing him, my tongue dancing along his as my hands clutched at his shirt.

He pulled back slightly, breaking the kiss, and grinned down at me. "I think we have an audience."

"Huh?" I jerked back and glanced around at all our friends staring at us, amused expressions on their faces. Heat crawled up my cheeks as mortification took over. What had I been thinking? "Oops."

Cheers and wolf whistles erupted around us, Pyper's the loudest of them all. Her hair was now all electric blue, and she'd painted her face white with black eyes and stitches from the sides of her mouth across her cheeks. She was the perfect zombie bride.

"Nice show," she said, slipping her arm through mine. "How in the world did you get him into a kilt? Damn, girl. Can't blame you for going all whore-of-the-damned on us with him looking like that."

Snickering, I snuck another glance at Kane. I didn't know why his bare knees were so damned sexy, but they were. "I might have mentioned something about a fantasy involving a highlander a week or two ago."

She shook her head. "If I didn't love you both so much, I'd have to stab you from pure jealousy."

I knew she was talking about the relationship Kane and I shared and not that she wanted Kane in any way. They'd dated once, way back in college, but she'd been the one to end it. Something about him being too conservative for her. Which was laughable, since conservative was the last word I'd use to describe him. But Pyper was ultra alternative in almost every area of her life, from her business choices, to her art, to the men she dated.

"What about you and Julius? What happened there?" I asked, now that she was all up in my business.

She shrugged. "No idea. One minute I was painting him, the next we were staring at each other, locked in that moment. You know the one. When everything stops and the only thing that exists is each other?"

I nodded. "Sure."

"Well, we were right there. And then I couldn't help it. The next thing I knew I was kissing him, and he was into it like a sex-starved man. Things were moving so fast and heated, we were moments from being naked and sweaty."

I widened my eyes. "Really? That's..."

"Stupid," she said. She clamped her mouth shut, her cheeks reddening. "We barely know each other, but there was this strange pull I couldn't step away from."

"Until we interrupted you and he bolted," I added.

"Yeah." She frowned. "Not my finest moment. Usually I'm much more professional."

I sent her a sidelong glance and smirked. "Well, your performance certainly didn't look amateurish to me, if you know what I mean."

Her frown disappeared, replaced by mock offense. "Are you sexually harassing me, Calhoun?"

I laughed and handed her one of the staff badges. "Not yet, but maybe later if we have time. Come on, let's get this party going."

CHAPTER 3

" *F*irst things first," I said, standing in the middle of the empty ballroom. "Seeing as how it's Halloween, I think it's imperative we cast a protection spell."

Lucien, my second-in-command and Kat's boyfriend, joined me. "I agree."

"Okay," Kane said. "What do you need us to do?"

"Be the points on our circle is all." I raised my hands, imagined a pentagram, and reached for my magical spark. It responded immediately. As I focused on the ground, I said, "*Illuminate.*"

A large, glowing pentagram appeared in the middle of the ballroom. I stood on the point facing north and waved for the others to take a spot. Pyper, Kat, Lucien, and Kane completed the points, even though Lucien was the only one with magic. It didn't matter for a simple protection spell.

Lucien and I met each other's gaze across the pentagram, and after I counted to three, we each unleashed magic within the circle. Our magical energy collided and mixed, slowly spreading out within the confines of the pentagram until the entire area glowed with magic. I raised my arms once more and said, "From point to point to person to person, may the gift of the coven watch over our guests tonight to keep them safe from evil forces. From person to person to point to point, may the night be full of fun and smart choices."

The combined magic from me and Lucien brightened, converged into a ball, rose high above us, and then burst like confetti into tiny specs of light all over the ballroom.

The magical pentagram vanished as a blanket of peace settled around us.

"Wow. Nice," Pyper said. "We should do that more often."

"Then what would we do for fun?" Kane asked, tugging me to his side. He winked at me. We both knew if true evil wanted in, there was no stopping it, but a protection spell would deflect any random acts of supernatural trouble.

Kat shook her head and smoothed her short skirt while we all laughed.

PYPER and I were behind the bar mixing drinks when Kat came running up, her face flushed. "Oh my God, look who's here again." She pointed across the room at Julius, who was standing around looking completely lost in his linen pants and smeared body paint.

"What the hell is he doing?" Pyper shoved a beer at one of the guests and ran out from behind the bar straight for him. A moment later, she was pulling him out of the party toward the meeting room where she'd painted the rest of the models.

"Do you think she needs help?" Kat asked.

Grinning, I shook my head. "I think she can handle him. Besides, there's too much to do out here. Can you check on the caterers? The food was supposed to start coming out of the kitchen ten minutes ago."

I waved at Kane's club manager, Charlie, who was talking to one of the three dancers. She nodded and strode over, dressed as a badass biker chick, her staff badge clipped to the bottom of her jacket. "Hey," I said. "I could use some help. Pyper got called away."

"Sure thing, gorgeous." She winked and turned to the next customer. "The dancers are set to get going in the next few minutes."

"Thanks." They were dressed as slutty angels and were going to dance in the cages high above the crowd just as soon as the theatrics started.

It took no time at all for Charlie and me to fall back into a regular working rhythm. I used to tend bar with her regularly at Wicked before Kane and I had gotten married. It was fun to be at it again.

"Hey, boss lady," Charlie said. "Looks like you've still got skills. Are you cheating on me tending bar somewhere else these days?"

"Yeah, right." I rolled my eyes. "And I'm not the boss. Cut it out."

"You are tonight." She jerked her head toward Kane, who appeared to be socializing more than anything. "Looks like the boss man is in his element."

I nodded. "It's one of his gifts." Ever since he'd been turned into an incubus, people of all walks of life were drawn to him. It was as if they couldn't get enough. And I couldn't blame them; I felt the same.

"Gift, right." Charlie snorted. "Lucky bastard."

That made me laugh as I poured half a dozen shots of tequila for the group standing in front of me.

Charlie smiled at a cute coed wearing a barely-there peacock outfit.

I turned to the next customer, but all the lights went out, leaving us in pitch-black darkness. The crowd gasped, and a scream came from the corner.

I glanced up and waited. The hallowed organ music filled the club, followed by three spotlights aimed at the three cages. Each angel was perfectly still in the moment. Then the music stopped for a beat, followed by the dramatic shift of Pink singing about getting the party started.

Soft lighting lit the room, and a cheer went through the crowd as the angels started to dance.

"Nice touch," Kat said, slipping behind the bar to grab a couple bottles of beer.

"Everything going okay?" I asked.

"Perfect." She nodded to the body-painted models making their way through the crowd, each carrying an appetizer tray. They were covered in an array of intricate designs, from a blooming forest with day-of-the-dead skulls, to gruesome vampire victims, to mutilated zombies. Pyper's skills were simply amazing.

I glanced back at the door where she'd disappeared with Julius and frowned. Was she okay? The thought sent a ripple of unease up my spine. Something wasn't right when it came to Julius, the way he'd disappeared and then returned so disoriented. Maybe he needed help?

I was just about to send Kane to check on them when Julius walked through the side door, Pyper close on his heels. His chest had been repainted with the skeleton hand appearing to rip out his heart, but his face had been left untouched, unlike the rest of the models. And damn if he didn't look even more handsome in the dim lighting. Who could blame Pyper for sticking with him? He had her hand tucked in his as he led her to the middle of the dance floor.

"Who's that?" Charlie asked.

I shrugged. "Some model named Julius."

"They look good together," she said.

They did. I couldn't keep my eyes off them. Julius placed one hand on her waist and held her hand with his other in a traditional dance stance. They stood facing each other for just a moment. And then they started to move.

The music suddenly cut from a popular Black Eyed Peas song to a fast song from the Roaring Twenties. The lights came up and shone on the makeshift dance floor.

"Whoa. Was that part of the plan?" Charlie asked me.

But I didn't say anything. I couldn't. I was too busy gawking at Julius and Pyper.

They had morphed from gruesome dead guy and zombie bride to a shiny, happy, swing-dancing couple from the twenties. The body paint was gone, replaced by Julius in a white suit and Pyper in a blue-and-white polka-dot dress.

"Oh my God," I heard Charlie whisper.

Then I tore my eyes from my friend and sucked in a hard breath as magic pooled automatically at my fingertips.

The center of the room had morphed into a nineteen-twenties dance party, and everyone on the dance floor along with it.

CHAPTER 4

I glanced down at myself. A rush of relief washed over me at the sight of my slutty devil outfit. Charlie hadn't changed either and was still clad in her biker leathers. "You see what I see, right?"

Her eyes were wide with disbelief. "You mean the roaring party that's going on and the fact that three-quarters of the guests are doing the Charleston?"

I nodded.

"Yeah. I see it. But I don't believe it." She glanced up at the former angels, who were now wearing flapper dresses and kicking their feet back as they danced with abandon to the new music.

I glanced around, looking for Lucien, and spotted the half-dozen body-painted models standing off to the side, gaping. A handful of other guests were transfixed, watching with interest.

"It's not magical," Lucien said from behind me.

I spun. "Are you sure?"

He nodded. "We'd feel a magical signature."

Of course we would. I was in the habit of closing down around too many people to protect myself. That meant I was working without one of my most powerful resources. I took a step back and released all my guards, letting all the emotions slam into me. Wonder, elation, joy, and an underlying trace of despair.

And as the music sped up, the despair intensified.

"Do you feel that?" I asked Lucien.

He took a step closer and peered at the dancers. "What?"

"Their pain."

He startled. "No."

Threads of hopelessness bubbled to the surface. I had to figure out a way to bring everyone back, to snap them out of this weird trance. My attention fixated on Pyper and Julius just as Julius twirled Pyper halfway across the dance floor, leaving a clear opening to see the rest of the dancers.

My heart all but stopped. Kane and Kat were right in the middle, dancing their hearts out. Both of them appeared to be having the time of their lives, seemingly oblivious to what had happened.

"Kat!" Lucien cried and tugged me out from behind the bar.

I went with him willingly, but stopped him before he could pull us onto the dance floor. "Wait."

He frowned. "For what?"

"We don't know if we'll be affected if we cross over. I think it might be better to try to break the..." Shoot. I was going to say "spell," but it wasn't one. Lucien was right. I couldn't feel even an ounce of magic radiating from the area. "Have you ever heard of a time warp?"

He shook his head. "No. You think that's what this is?"

"I don't know. It's not a spell." I circled the wooden stage until I was closer to Kat and Kane. Then I called, "Kane!"

No answer.

"Kat!" Lucien waved, trying to get her attention.

Neither noticed us. No one did.

The rest of the guests were gathering around us, moving closer to the dancers. Even Charlie. They were moving toward the stage as if they were in a trance, not at all disturbed by the turn of events.

"Charlie?" I asked, touching her arm.

She shrugged me off and kept moving.

"Hey, Charlie. No!"

But it was no use. She stepped up onto the stage. As soon as she crossed the plane, her clothes switched from badass biker bitch to sweet swing dancer with jeweled high heels. My eyes bugged out. I'd never seen Charlie in anything other than jeans and formfitting T-shirts. Dresses were definitely not her thing.

Before long, every last person in the ballroom had crossed into the time warp except for me and Lucien.

We met each other's gazes.

"Should we call the coven?" I asked Lucien.

"Probably, but they aren't going to be able to get here anytime soon. The crowds and traffic tonight are nearly as bad as during Mardi Gras."

He had a point. All of us who were here either lived in the French Quarter or were staying over with someone who did. The parking and traffic would be awful right now. Still, I'd call if I had to, but I wasn't even sure what any of us could do, if anything.

I pulled my phone out and called my mentor Bea.

"Happy Halloween, Jade," she said cheerfully. "What can I do for you?"

"Thank the Goddess," I said and took a step away from the stage. "We seem to have a situation here."

She let out a low laugh. "It's Halloween. Of course you do."

"Bea," I said. "It's not funny. We seem to have some sort of a time warp going on. We're putting on a party for one of Pyper's clients, and suddenly everyone on the dance floor shifted to some weird alternate reality from the nineteen twenties. They're wearing period clothing, their hairstyles are totally different, and the music that's playing isn't from our sound system. It's like a worm hole or something."

"Magic?" she asked.

"Neither Lucien nor I can feel anything."

"Are there any spirits present?"

It was a reasonable question and one I should've thought about. We were in the French Quarter, where practically every building was haunted. "Possibly, though I don't see any."

Bea sighed in exasperation. "Jade, it's about time you start to use your gifts instead of running from them."

I clamped my lips shut, knowing she was talking about my empath gift. I'd spent the majority of my childhood trying to forget I could read people. I had kept it a secret from everyone I could, because when I read someone's emotions, it made both of us uncomfortable. It was an intrusion of epic proportions. So it was usually my last resort, especially in highly charged situations like a party. I'd already opened up once, but hadn't probed too deeply, nor had I wanted to.

"Use your gift to find the spirit. Then you and Lucien can

cast a spell to isolate him or her. Everyone else should snap back into reality." She said all of this in a matter-of-fact tone as if we weren't in the middle of an emergency situation. Compared to demons and black magic, I supposed we weren't. But it was still worrisome.

"Isolation spell. Got it. Thanks," I said.

"And, Jade?"

"Yes, Bea?"

"Try not to trap anyone in the past."

"Funny." Although, I didn't think her comment was meant as a joke. "Sorry. I'm a little tense. Can I call if we need more help?"

"Yes, but I'm not even in town, so if you need backup, call Lailah." She was referring to our resident angel who was in charge of keeping souls safe.

"Okay. Thanks." I hit END and trotted back over to Lucien. He hadn't moved as he kept a close eye on Kat.

"She looks upset," he said.

I nodded. "There's a weird undercurrent of desperation and despair coming from the dance floor. But I can't tell who it's coming from. More than one person, I think. It might be spreading like a cancer."

His fists clenched in frustration. "What did Bea say?"

"She suspects a spirit might be anchoring everyone to the past. If we can figure out who it is, we can isolate him or her with a spell and then this could be over in a few minutes."

We both turned and stared at the crowd. Because this was a party we were hired to plan, we didn't know most of the guests. I wasn't even sure if the host was here yet. Bea had said to use my gift, and it appeared that was exactly what I was going to have to do.

"I'm going to start reading people. If I look like I'm going to pass out, take my hand, okay?" I said.

Lucien nodded. He knew that once I opened my senses and took on everyone else's emotional energy, I'd be toasted emotionally and physically. But if I could focus on one person, especially someone I knew well, I'd be okay.

I cast Lucien one last glance and then braced myself as I focused on Kane. At first all I got was a shot of humor, followed by elation. But as I slipped past his barriers, the happiness slowly faded away and I was left with a cold emptiness. As if his soul was missing or buried.

My heart sped up, and my entire body went cold with fear. Kane. No. This couldn't be happening.

"Jade? What's wrong?" I heard Lucien ask.

But I didn't answer. I was too horrified by what I was sensing. Kane wasn't really in there. He was like a shell of a person, with superficial happiness radiating from him. As if whoever or whatever was pulling the strings wanted everyone to appear normal when really they were being sucked into an abyss.

I didn't want to let go of my hold on Kane. It was too painful, too awful, but I had to find out if he was the only one affected or if everyone was being pulled under.

With great reluctance, I shifted my focus from Kane to Kat. And although her emotional signature was completely different, her emotions felt exactly the same as Kane's. Superficially happy and elated, but underneath, there was nothing. Not even a twinge of hope, or sadness, or reluctance. Nothing.

Frantic, I hopped from person to person, experiencing the same lack of emotions, the same zombified dancers... until I got to Pyper.

Wonder radiated off her as she stared into Julius's eyes, followed by a small underlying trace of trepidation. But she wasn't fearful. No, more like cautious, as if she was afraid what she was feeling wouldn't last. I focused on her smiling face and did my best to shut out all the artificial joy that was overwhelming the rest of the dancers. All I wanted was Pyper's emotions.

Hope. Nervousness. Curiosity. Desire. They were all there, swirling around her in a thick cloud.

I opened my eyes and peered at Julius. His expression was soft, tender as he watched my friend stare into his eyes. But as I tried to penetrate his senses, once I pushed through the initial spark of hope, I was overwhelmed with deep-seated hopelessness and despair. All the negative emotions permeating the room were coming from him. His emotions were disconcerting, but they were real. Just like Pyper's, but unlike everyone else's.

What was different about the two of them? Why did they each have their own emotions when no one else did? Was something sinister infecting everyone else and not them?

But I hadn't felt anything sinister. Nothing even close to evil, except the apparent lack of soul from everyone else in the crowd.

"I don't know what to do," I said abruptly to Lucien.

"What do you mean? Have you found the spirit yet?"

"No. I mean, I'm not sure." I kept my gaze on Pyper and Julius. Pyper certainly wasn't a spirit. And Julius was clearly a solid man. All the ghosts I'd met before had been apparitions. All of them except Camille, who'd managed to possess people to take on a form. My stomach rolled with unease. "Oh, no. I think it's Julius."

"You think?"

I nodded. "I'm not too sure. All I know is Pyper and Julius are the only ones with real emotions there. Everyone else is in a trance. And I can't sense any other emotional energy like I usually can when ghosts are present but not visible. I know Pyper isn't a ghost. Her emotional signature hasn't changed. I'd recognize her anywhere. That leaves Julius as the odd man out."

"No one. Not any of the servers or guests?"

I shook my head, more and more convinced. "No one. Julius disappeared today and then came back out of the blue. No one knows where he came from. And add in the fact that this all started right after Pyper and Julius started dancing. It has to be him."

"Okay, then. I trust you." Lucien held his hand out to me. "Let's go get him."

I glanced around, trying to calm the panic setting in. I had no idea what was going to happen once we stepped onto the dance floor. But we couldn't isolate Julius from here. We had to separate him from Pyper first.

Blowing out a breath, I took Lucien's hand in mine, and together the pair of us crossed the plane into the nineteen-twenties.

CHAPTER 5

A flash of heat washed over me and then my body went completely numb. But I didn't seem to care. Life was free. Happy. Full of celebration. I turned to Lucien. "Care to dance?"

He inclined his head, bowed slightly, then swept me up in the music. My feet seemed to move on their own. All I saw was Lucien's smiling face and flashes of color as he twirled me around and around among the other dancers.

The music played on one continual loop, never pausing, and soon enough, although I didn't want to sit the dance out, my limbs became heavy. But no matter how much I wanted to stop to take a breath, my limbs wouldn't respond to my mental commands. And worse, I couldn't keep the smile off my face.

I was trapped in a dancing hell, along with the rest of my friends and all the other party guests. My eyes met Lucien's.

He had the same manic expression on his face I feared was on mine. But his eyes were searching mine, silently asking me the same thing I was asking myself. How did we end up here? I wasn't sure. All I knew was we needed to stop. To get a drink. To do something other than move our feet.

With my limbs not responding, I gathered the ball of magic that lived just below my heart and sent it shooting toward my fingers.

The magic erupted from my fingertips like a bolt of lightning, knocking both me and Lucien backward. We each landed on our backsides, gawking at each other.

"What the hell was that, Jade?" Lucien said, jumping to his feet to loom over me.

I smiled up at him and pushed myself to my feet. "A wake-up call." I waved a hand around the dance floor. "We were stuck just like they are."

His expression turned blank as his gaze lingered on the fatigued dancers. Then recognition lit in his clear green eyes. "Damn. We were sucked right in, weren't we?"

I nodded and moved to the side to avoid being kicked by one of the dancers. "We need to get to Julius."

"Can't we just zap everyone out of their state?"

I glanced down at my white cotton dress and black Mary Jane pumps, noting my devil outfit was nowhere to be found. I shook my head. "It doesn't look like we've left this reality, does it?"

"No, but—"

"Besides, we don't know everyone's tolerance for a magical electric shock. It was okay for you and me, but we're witches. They aren't."

He fixated on Kat, who was off to our right, and furrowed his brow. The worry clinging to him brushed up against my psyche. I wanted to put a hand on his arm, do or say something to comfort him, but I had no words. And I wasn't completely sure that we wouldn't end up like dancing monkeys again if we touched.

I was just as upset about what was happening to Kat as he was. She was my best friend. And then there was Kane. He was a demon hunter. If Hell had found some way to take his soul, if that was why I couldn't reach him, then... I couldn't even think about it. The situation would be too awful.

"We need to separate Julius from Pyper," I said.

"How?" Lucien studied the other man, his eyes narrowed.

"Ask to cut in, and I'll invoke the spell?" I wasn't at all confident that would work, as the pair seemed to only have eyes for each other, but it was worth a shot.

"I'll try." Lucien took a step forward and then paused. "Zap me if I go back into zombie mode."

"Will do."

The one thing about being in the time warp was that emotions weren't really a huge issue at the moment. Joy and happiness actually filled me up, gave me a bit of a boost for a while until they wore me out. Even the fake kind. It was everything else, such as anger, depression, and sadness, that turned me into a basket case.

Lucien hovered around Pyper and Julius, and finally when Julius twirled her into his body and paused for a moment, Lucien moved in, placing a hand on the small of Pyper's back. She froze and slowly twisted her head to glance at him.

"May I cut in, miss?" He half bowed just as he'd done to me, and suddenly I was certain his memory had been wiped clean again. But when he pulled Pyper into his arms, almost against her will, he winked at me and led her awkwardly toward the other side of the dance floor.

Relief flooded me. He'd only been acting the part.

Julius stared after them, a storm of emotion in his dark eyes. I saw the cloud of rage encompass him before I felt it. Pure hatred. Dark anger. The kinds of emotions that make men commit horrible sins. And it was all directed at Lucien.

"Whoa," I said to myself, gathering every last ounce of magic I could grab onto. He needed to be isolated, and fast. A small twinge of longing for the help of Bea or the coven hit me, but I knew I could do this. I'd fought worse and won. I could take on one spirit.

I imagined the pentagram I'd conjured earlier in the day, only smaller, and as Julius moved past me toward Pyper, I pushed my hands out, aiming for his feet. The pentagram lit on the floor exactly where I'd intended. And Julius was smack in the middle of it.

"*Capiantur!*" I cried.

The light from the pentagram shot straight up out of the ground, imprisoning Julius within the circle.

The music cut off abruptly, and all the dancing stopped. A punishing wave of relief slammed into me as a fair number of the guests sank to their knees, winded from their manic dancing.

I glanced toward Kane and Kat, triumph strumming through me. Kat was clutching her side, leaning into Kane. He was frowning and wiping his brow. He hadn't seen me yet, but that was okay. I took a step toward them and then stopped dead in my tracks.

No one was dancing. The music was gone. But everyone was still in their nineteen-twenties outfits and the gaslights were still burning brightly, despite the fact they were no longer operational in our own time.

We should've morphed back to the twenty-first century

but we hadn't. We were still stuck in the time warp. At least people seemed to have their senses back for the most part.

"Move!" Lucien called. "Get off the dance floor. Everyone. Go now."

The group of partygoers did as he asked and retreated from the stage. As each person left, I caught a glimpse of their outfits morphing back into their Halloween costumes as they disappeared into the fading darkness surrounding the dance floor.

"Go on now," I said to a coed and her date. "Drinks are at the bar." Her date's eyes lit with interest, and the pair slipped back to where they belonged.

I was making my way through the crowd toward Kane and Kat when Pyper's energy invaded mine, sending fear and pure disgust up my spine. I spun in her direction and froze.

Roy, an evil ghost we'd once sent to Hell after he'd tortured both me and Pyper, had his arm around her neck, locking her in a chokehold. Only he wasn't solid. He was sort of translucent, which told me everything he was doing was fueled by stolen energy. But whose?

With my palms sparking with magic, I cried, "Let her go."

"Not likely, white witch. But I'll consider it, if you give me what I want." He chuckled, his laugh low and sinister. "Nice try with the protection spell. A lesser spirit would've had trouble with that one."

My body shook with uncontrollable anger. I wanted nothing more than to blast his ass into a million pieces. Only he was likely to just evaporate, considering his nonsolid form. I'd try it anyway, except he was using Pyper as a shield. I'd have to bide my time. "What is it you want, you sick bastard?"

He jerked his head toward Kane, who was a few feet

away, barely being held back by Kat. She was whispering furiously in his ear, both hands clutched around his arm. "Give me his soul, and I'll leave this one alone." Roy tightened his grip around Pyper's throat until her eyes bugged out from lack of oxygen.

"Never going to happen," I said, sounding braver than I actually felt. I was fortified by the knowledge that Kane's energy was back, and I felt every inch of his being straight down to my toes. He'd never been soulless.

Pyper was trying to claw at Roy's arm, but there wasn't anything there for her to grab. He was choking her using pure energy. "Let Pyper go, or else I'm going to let Kane end you for good."

Roy cast Kane a sideways glance, the same dark anger that had been surrounding Julius radiating from him. Only it was stronger. Darker. Angrier. The cloud hadn't been coming from Julius. It had been coming from Roy. He'd been here the entire time and had somehow been attached to Julius. Roy jabbed his head toward Kane. "You think that one's going to take me down? Right. All he was ever good at was throwing a punch. And as you can see, that's not going to work this time."

"Think again," Kane said, shrugging Kat off. He lifted his arm, holding his hand out. A flash of light shot from his palm, and when it died down, his demon-hunter dagger lay in his open hand, the intricate symbol on the handle glowing blue.

Roy's gaze locked on Kane's hand. Fear flashed over his features. A second later, his expression went blank. "Forget it. I'll take hers." He jerked Pyper back, indicating he'd steal her soul instead.

"No way, asshole," I spat out and then did the only thing I

could think of. I launched myself at them, taking Pyper down in a heap of limbs.

She coughed and curled into a ball, rubbing at her throat.

I scrambled to my feet, magic pulsing in my fingers, ready to fight.

But Roy had vanished.

CHAPTER 6

"Pyper!" I dropped to her side, gently taking one of her hands. "Are you all right?"

She sucked in a breath and then pushed herself up, her eyes ablaze with fury. "Where is he?"

"I don't know. He's gone." I brushed her hair out of her eyes, but she shook me off.

"No. He isn't. I still feel him. His ugly hatred, it's here. He won't leave until he gets what he wants." She climbed to her feet, glanced around, and fixated on the light still shining from the pentagram. "Is Julius still in there?"

I nodded. "He somehow trapped us in a time warp."

She shook her head. "No, he didn't. That was Roy."

"What?"

Kane joined me by my side. "What do you mean?"

"Let him out," Pyper demanded. "Now."

I glanced at Lucien. He raised his hands in an I-don't-know motion.

"Jade!" Pyper turned and grabbed my shoulders. "Let him out. He's in danger in there."

She was so frantic, so insistent, I did as she asked. With a wave of my hand, the light vanished, and Julius stood in the middle of the pentagram, watching us. Nothing changed. The music didn't come back on. No one started dancing as they had earlier. But we still hadn't morphed back to our own time.

"What's going on?" I heard Kat ask Lucien.

Pyper took two steps toward Julius and then froze, her eyes never leaving his. "Where is he?"

Julius stared over her shoulder, hatred pouring out of his dark gaze. "Right behind you."

Pyper whirled, narrowed her eyes, and said, "Show yourself, you coward."

Nothing happened.

"Pyper, we should probably leave and go back to our time. All we need to do is walk off this dance floor," I said.

"No." She placed her hands on her hips, fierce determination radiating off her. "Not until we finish Roy. He won't leave me alone. Not now that he has an in."

"An in?" I asked her.

She glanced at Julius. "He's a ghost, you know."

I nodded. "Yes, I thought he might be, but he's unusual being in solid form and all."

She nodded. "He was a witch."

"Ohhh," Kat said as if that explained everything.

"A white witch." Pyper met my gaze. "A powerful one, like you. And for some reason, Roy's latched on to him. I don't know why or how, but I can feel it."

I glanced at Julius and back at her. They were gazing at each other with a curious intensity. "Today isn't the first time you two met, is it?"

Pyper glanced away, a blush creeping up her face.

"Pyper?" Kane asked, his curious tone tinged with concern.

"No. It is not," Julius said rather formally. "I had the pleasure of meeting Miss Pyper not long ago when she was helping another research this hotel."

We all turned and gaped at Pyper.

But before anyone could say anything, Julius's head and upper body jerked back as if he'd suffered a blow. He let out a grunt and came up swinging, but appeared to only find air.

"Roy!" Pyper called and jumped forward.

Kane clasped a hand over her arm, pulling her back with him. "Stay by my side."

"But I can't let him go after Julius. You don't understand. He feeds off of Julius's energy."

Her words clicked a switch in my brain. I could find him. If I tuned in to Julius, I'd know exactly where Roy was. "Lucien?"

"Yes?"

I waved him over and whispered into his ear. "I need to invade Julius's energy. When I give the signal, I need you to cast a summoning spell."

"Without a circle?"

"Yes. Once you cast the spell and I direct the energy to it, I'll call the circle myself."

He gave me a skeptical look.

"Trust me."

"You got it, boss."

With Pyper safely at Kane's side, I threw my energy into Julius, instantly honing in on Roy tapping into him. I'd once been a victim of Roy's wrath and unfortunately knew his energy intimately. It didn't take much to follow that thread. And as I did, I severed the hold Roy had on Julius. It was just me and Roy now. In order for him to stay connected to our world, he had to siphon magic from me. Except I had no intention of letting him. Once he reached for my energy, I sent a bolt of magic straight into his energy, effectively latching on, and then wrapped him in an invisible binding. He wasn't going anywhere now. Not until I was sure we were sending him somewhere where he could no longer get to Pyper.

And even though I was stronger now, had better control over my gifts, the dark taint of Roy's shriveled soul made my skin crawl and my insides shudder from the pure filth that was Roy.

But I wasn't going to let him get the better of me. Not this time. As hard as it was, I forced myself to take steps toward the middle of the dance floor, toward the ugliest being I'd ever come in contact with, and that was saying something.

My movements became slower and slower with each step, my limbs like cement pillars, refusing to move. And when I was certain I was going to collapse from the sheer pain of holding on to Roy, I felt a hand slip into mine. Pyper's cool, clean, refreshing energy rushed into my being, fortifying me, giving me the strength to hold on.

I felt Roy's rage, his frustration at being locked in my magical hold, but clung to Pyper's sure determination and cried, "Lucien, now!"

The low murmur of his Latin chant filled the silence, and a second later, I felt him let his magic go. Through our coven connection, I guided it, forcing it to hit exactly where I knew Roy was standing. And then as his form came into view, I raised my arms and called the pentagram.

Pure white light filled the ballroom, nearly blinding me.

"Whoa," I heard Kat gasp. "That was impressive."

Glancing down, I smiled in sheer satisfaction. Pyper and I were standing on the northernmost point of the pentagram, and Roy was trapped in the innermost circle. Exactly as I'd planned.

"Nice work," Lucien said.

"Thanks. You, too. But it's not over yet. What should we do with Roy?"

"I'll take care of him," Kane said, moving to stand just behind me.

I turned my head and raised a curious eyebrow. "Really? And how do you propose to do that?"

"Like this." He palmed the hilt of his dagger, and in one swift motion he threw the magical blade right at Roy, hitting him exactly where his heart would be. Roy vanished, and the dagger hung in the air for a few seconds.

Then Roy reappeared for just an instant and shattered into tiny slivers of light that faded away before they ever hit the ground.

CHAPTER 7

$\mathcal{T}$he white light and the pentagram vanished as the lights dimmed and Maroon 5 blared from the sound system. My friends turned from nineteen-twenties swing dancers to sexified Halloween revelers.

Lucien strode over to Kat and gathered her in his arms, while Kane, sporting his kilt, wrapped one arm around me and his other around Pyper. But she was staring at Julius.

He stood by himself, watching her, a wistful expression on his face. "He's gone."

Pyper nodded.

"For good this time."

"Yeah."

We were standing in the packed party, surrounded by partygoers, and yet I felt as if I was intruding on something deeply personal. I tucked my hand into Kane's and gently tugged him back. "I think they might need a moment," I whispered to him.

He glanced down at me and frowned. "He's a ghost. I don't think—"

"You don't need to think," I said mildly. "He isn't dangerous."

Instinctively, I knew my words were true. Earlier I hadn't been able to feel anything radiating from Julius, but I did now. There was only goodness and love and regret.

Kane reluctantly took a step back with me as we watched Pyper move toward Julius as if she was mystically drawn to him in some way. And when she stopped in front of him, he smiled down at her, cupped her cheek, and whispered something in her ear.

She shook her head slowly and placed her hand over the exploding heart she'd drawn on his chest. The sadness radiating off them just about brought tears to my eyes. Pyper rose to her tiptoes and pressed a soft kiss to Julius's lips. They were frozen in the moment, the perfect zombie couple, and then Julius faded away. And Pyper was left alone in the middle of the ballroom.

She stood there, her shoulders slumped and her head inclined.

"Excuse me," I said to Kane and hurried to Pyper's side. I placed a hand on her shoulder. "Hey, you. Let's get out of here."

She shook her head, still staring straight ahead. "We have work to do."

I made a show of glancing around. "Na. Kane and Charlie have everything under control. We're free to do anything we want. Including grabbing a bottle of tequila and doing shots until we pass out."

"Tempting," she said dryly. "But maybe just a few beers."

"You got it." We walked together to the bar, where I grabbed four beers and a bottle opener. I waited a beat for Charlie to finish mixing a few drinks. The night's events hadn't fazed her at all. She was back at work, flirting with males and females alike, raking in the tips as always. "We'll be in the meeting room just outside the ballroom if you need us."

She gave Pyper a sympathetic smile. "Sure, but I'll be fine."

"I know you will."

I handed one of the beers to Pyper and followed her out of the room.

We slipped into the adjoining room, and instead of sitting on the chairs lining the wall, Pyper walked to the middle of the room and sank to the floor.

I joined her and watched as she downed half her beer.

"Better?" I asked.

She shook her head. "Not really."

"Roy is gone. That dagger of Kane's is magical. He won't be coming back."

She nodded. "I know." Glancing up at me, she pierced me with a flat stare. "I wasn't afraid of him, you know. Roy, I mean."

I jerked back slightly at her remark. "Really? I was."

"No you weren't. You were worried about everyone, but you weren't afraid of him. Not this time."

She was right. I'd been afraid for her, afraid of anything she was feeling, but with Kane and Lucien there, I hadn't been frightened by Roy. Only concerned with how best to get rid of him. Luckily Kane had found his opening. "Okay, but I did have a minor anxiety attack when he first showed up. Any ideas on how that happened?"

She grimaced. "I didn't know he was a ghost at first, you know."

I frowned, confused.

"Julius. You didn't either."

"Damn," I said under my breath. "You're right. I didn't. Why didn't you say something?"

Her face got even brighter red. "I was going to. Later."

"Later? Later than what? How long have you two known each other, really?"

She hesitated and stared at her hands. "You know since Ian's been gone, I've gotten into hunting ghosts as a hobby. Well, he showed up at an investigation about a month ago. And then at the two after that."

"He moves around?" That was unusual for ghosts. Mostly they haunted specific places.

"He was a witch."

"So?"

She shrugged. "The rules are different for him. He can pop in and out of wherever he wants to, but his time is limited. He only has so much energy, you know."

I wanted to ask about the relationship they'd obviously started, but I didn't know how to broach it. Instead I asked, "And what about Roy? Do you have any idea why he showed up here tonight? Or what happened with the time warp?"

"I...oh, damn. Julius said he wanted to have just one dance from his own time. But seeing as it's Halloween and forces are, I don't know, different I suppose, his spell didn't quite work the way he intended. We were just supposed to slip into the twenties for one song and then back, but then that bastard Roy showed up and leeched his energy. It wasn't supposed to affect anyone else. I'm so sorry, Jade. It was an accident."

I heard what she said, and though it was unnerving she seemed to be having a romantic interlude with a ghost, who was I to judge? I'd had one once with a ghost who'd invaded my dreams. At the moment, I was more concerned with the evil spirit I'd thought we'd sent to Hell over a year ago. "Any idea where Roy came from?"

"No." Her answer was final, leaving no room for doubt she was telling the truth. She took a long swig of her beer and flopped backward on the floor, staring up at the ceiling. "No idea at all."

"I do," a male voice said from our left.

I jerked and caught sight of Julius's outline. He was only an apparition hovering just above the floor.

Pyper rose from her position on the floor and faced him, her head tilted to one side. "You're back."

"Sort of. But not for long."

I took in his long pants, suspenders, and sports coat. If I didn't know he was a product of the twenties, I might assume he was a hipster. He was certainly cute enough, if he wasn't a spirit, that was.

"I felt that other spirit a couple of weeks ago when you were investigating one of the big hotels. I didn't think about it much, because being a witch, spirits are attracted to my energy and try to feed off it. That's what this Roy did. I deal with it by shutting myself down, making my energy unavailable to them, and they usually go away. Except he happened to catch me off guard tonight. As soon as I realized he was here, I cut off my lingering magic, and that's what caused us to get stuck back in time. My apologies to everyone."

That would explain why I hadn't been able to feel many emotions. Julius's odd ghost magic had suppressed them, all except his and Pyper's, which were running really close to the surface. It was also why I couldn't feel his magic. Or it could just be because he's a ghost. Hard to say. "So he's been hanging around you lately, and because he saw an opening, he tried to take Kane's soul? Or someone else's so he could live again?"

Julius nodded. "Yes. Considering his fascination with Pyper, I suspect he'd been watching her for some time. But because of whatever y'all did to him last year, he didn't have the resources to get to her. And, well, now he's nothing."

Pyper climbed to her feet and walked over to where Julius was floating. The way they looked at each other made me feel as if I was intruding, but I had more questions.

"If Roy was in another dimension or in Hell, could he have still latched on to you?"

He nodded. "Yes. When I'm strong, spirits can and do try to infiltrate my energy. It's a burden, but usually I deal with it better. My apologies, Mrs. Rouquette. It won't happen again."

I had experience with attracting unsavory beings while not being able to control my magic as well as I'd hoped. And considering he was a ghost and not completely in control of his fate, I had some sympathy for him. Being a witch never got easier. "No apology needed, Julius. Sorry we thought it was you causing all the problems. I had no idea Roy was on the loose. Thank you for watching over Pyper. If our paths cross again, please consider us friends."

He bowed. "It will be my pleasure."

I smiled and waved as I left, giving them some privacy.

When I got back to the party, Pyper's client was on stage introducing his new band. Kane was standing near the bar, nursing a beer.

"Hey, highlander," I said, walking up behind Kane.

He turned and his sour expression vanished, replaced by one of concern. "Hey, pretty witch. How's Pyper?"

"She's just fine."

"You sure about that?" He glanced over my shoulder toward the side door.

"I'm positive. She's taking a moment to...ah...relax. I'm sure she'll be along in a few minutes." I ran my hand lightly down his chest, ready for some quality time with my man. "Care for a spin on the dance floor?"

His lips turned up into a slow smile. "Only if the devil comes out to play."

"Be careful what you wish for," I said, wrapping my arms around his neck. "You don't want to be classified as a sinner, do you?"

His heated gaze traveled the length of my body. "I think I'll risk it."

Then he pulled me to the dance floor, and the only thing left on my mind was Kane and that damned kilt. I placed my hands on his hips, curling my fingers into the rough fabric. "Think you might be willing to wear this once a week?"

His heated gaze dropped to my exposed cleavage. "If you wear that, I'm game."

"Deal," I said breathlessly. "Halloween, every Friday night."

His gaze met mine, and we both laughed.

"Well, maybe not Halloween, but kilts and corsets," I amended.

"You got it." He clutched me to him, pressing his hard body into mine. "Now kiss me."

And when our lips touched, a spark of magic zipped from me to him, sealing the deal.

***

Get the next Jade Calhoun book: Bewitched on Bourbon Street (Jade Calhoun Series, Book 7).

Join Deanna's reader group on Facebook.

To learn about Deanna's new releases sign up for her newsletter here. Do you prefer text alerts? Text WITCHYBOOKS to 24587 for news and updates.

Dear Reader, Reviews are always appreciated. Did you love this book? Please take a moment to let others know in the form of a review on your favorite vendor. XOXO, Deanna

A MIRACLE ON BOURBON STREET

It's Christmas Eve and Jade Calhoun's ready for a quiet, magical night with her husband Kane. But when Santa demons and energy-stealing elves start wreaking havoc, it's going to take a miracle on Bourbon Street to save Christmas.

CHAPTER 1

The soothing scents of molasses and cinnamon filled my kitchen as I pulled the gingerbread cake out of the oven. Perfect. The only thing left to do was to change into my Christmas witch outfit. The sexy one I'd picked out just for Kane.

It was Christmas Eve, and it had been well over a month since I'd spent any quality time with my gorgeous husband. We'd both been too busy: Kane hunting rogue demons and me rescuing lost souls from the shadow world. In the weeks between Halloween and Christmas, I'd personally saved forty-two souls from being snatched into Hell. We deserved a break.

And a little sexy time, hence the red velvet miniskirt and thigh-high boots waiting for me in my closet.

I smiled to myself and went to change. Thirty minutes later, I reemerged with my long strawberry blond hair tucked under a pointy red hat and wearing the sexified Mrs. Claus dress. Sparkling diamond pentagrams hung from my ears to complete the effect.

A knock sounded on the front door, followed by the creak of the hinges as someone let themselves in. "Jade?"

"Pyper?" I called back, striding from the kitchen in the back of our Victorian shotgun double toward the front of the house. She had a key, so it wasn't unusual for her to walk in, but she knew I had a romantic evening planned. Something was wrong.

Pyper, wearing a shimmering, silver-beaded dress, met me halfway in the dining room. "Oh, good. You're here."

"Where else would I be?" I glanced at the clock. "Kane's supposed to be here any minute."

She winced and a lock of her black and electric-blue-streaked hair fell over one eye. "No where, I just... sorry. I'm a little flustered. He was at the café when Santa showed up and tried to snag one of my customers."

"What? Someone tried to abduct a customer?" Pyper owned the Grind, a café on Bourbon Street. Usually the most troubling thing that happened there was her resident ghost drawing inappropriate sketches of éclairs and rum balls on the menu board.

"Not a someone. A demon," she said, her tone apologetic. "Kane went after him, obviously, but not before he sent me to—" The doorbell rang and she gave me a sheepish smile. "Well, you'll see. Come on."

I followed her to the door, but just before she slipped out, she swept her gaze down my body. "Super fun outfit, but I think you're gonna want your coat."

While New Orleans wasn't exactly freezing in December, it wasn't warm either. Wandering around in a miniskirt at night would turn me into a popsicle. "But I don't have anything that matches."

She rolled her eyes. "Can't you just spell something? You *are* a white witch."

"No. That would take a potion and a bunch of time. It's usually easier and more cost-effective to just buy something new." I sighed and reached for my new teal trench coat hanging on my coat rack.

Her lips twitched. "Uh, Jade, maybe white would be better."

"Of course it would, but it's at the cleaners. It's teal or nothing."

"Teal it is," she said, chuckling as she shuffled me out onto my front porch.

"What's this?" I asked, smiling. Sitting in front of my house was a horse-drawn carriage draped with holly and elaborate red ribbons.

"A pre-Christmas gift from Kane. He was going to take you on a ride around the Quarter to check out the holiday decorations. But since he's battling evil he sent me."

My heart swelled. What a sweet idea.

She climbed in the carriage and held up a thermos. "And there's hot buttered rum to get the party started."

"That will warm me up." I grinned and climbed in after her. "But where's the driver?"

She pumped her eyebrows and said, "Onward, Poindexter."

The horse, a real one, not the mules that carried the tourists around the French Quarter, lifted his head high and trotted forward.

"Poindexter?" I asked.

"He's the ghost steering the horse."

The carriage rolled along the paved streets and suddenly lit up with twinkle lights. Two mugs appeared out of thin air as the thermos levitated and poured a healthy dose into each mug.

I held my hand out and my grin widened as I turned to Pyper. "Did Kane set this all up by himself or did you help him?"

"I might have had a hand in it." She waved toward the seemingly empty driver's bench where the ghost must be. "Being a medium comes in handy sometimes. But Bea spelled the lights, mugs, and thermos."

A group effort then. Kane had gone through a lot of trouble and hadn't even been able to join me. I glanced down at my Mrs. Claus outfit and sighed. It would've been one hell of a Christmas Eve.

"Hey," Pyper said, putting her hand on my arm. "Don't count me out yet. We're going to have a hell of a time tonight."

"Of course we are." I raised my mug in a toast. "To the most fun a girl can have with her underwear on."

She burst out laughing. When she sobered, she gave me a sly smile. "Who said I was wearing underwear?"

"Oh, geez." I chuckled and took a long sip of my drink. "Figures. So, Miss Commando, where are we headed?"

Her eyes twinkled with mischief. "You'll see."

CHAPTER 2

$\mathcal{T}$he carriage rolled along the neighborhood streets of the Quarter and paused at a large private residence. The Creole townhouse that sat on the corner of Royal and St. Ann had a large wraparound balcony on both the second and third stories, each draped in garland filled with thousands of white twinkling lights. A dozen nutcrackers were on the second story balcony, positioned between the floor-to-ceiling windows, while two stood guard on the corner near the front door.

"Very pretty," I said, eyeing the huge holly wreaths hanging in each of the windows. Gorgeous crystal bulbs hung in the middle of the wreaths and sparkled from the twinkle lights.

"Yeah, it is. But watch this." She nodded to the house with a coy smile.

"Watch what—Oh!" Music from *The Nutcracker*, "Dance of the Sugar Plum Fairy," filled the streets, and the giant wooden nutcrackers came to life. They stepped forward, moving their arms up and down in time with the music. Then the lights started to blink, also in time with the music.

I was transfixed as I sat there with the cup of hot buttered rum warming my hands. The tingle of magic in the air was comforting, familiar, and I knew at once Bea, my mentor, had been responsible for the spell. A crowd had gathered, their happiness filling me up, making me whole on the most wonderful night of the year. Sometimes it wasn't so bad being an empath. On nights like Christmas Eve when everyone was hopeful and loving, it was nothing short of miraculous.

"Kane set this up?" I asked Pyper, watching the crystal ornaments change from red to green to silver.

"Yeah. You must be really good in bed to deserve this." She winked and raised her mug, saluting me.

"You did not just say that." I laughed and turned my attention back to the magical Christmas show. When the song ended, the nutcrackers marched back to their starting point and the lights winked out. The crowd erupted in excited applause, once again boosting my energy.

A small twinge of sadness hit me as I longed for Kane to be sitting beside me. He'd gone out of his way to make the night special for me, and he was missing it.

Pyper patted my knee. "Cheer up, Jade. I'm sure he'll catch up with us as soon as he can."

I glanced at her. "Are you the empath now?"

"Ha. Hardly. But there's no mistaking that wistfulness in your puppy dog eyes. Now stop moping. We have six more stops."

"Seriously?"

"Yep." She waved a hand. "Onward, Poindexter."

The horse trotted forward, and once again, we were on

the move. We stopped at five more houses, and each one put on an awe inspiring show: singing sugar plums, spinning Christmas trees, animated snowmen, dancing candy canes, and tumbling gingerbread men. By the time the carriage turned in through the gates of Jackson Square Park in the French Quarter, I was certain we'd seen everything; that is until I spotted the parade making its way along the paved paths, being led by twelve drummers drumming. Behind them was a gaggle of eleven men in kilts carrying bagpipes.

I pointed with my mouth open. "Kane did that too?"

Pyper laughed. "No. That's the entertainment for the lighting of the Christmas tree."

There was a giant tree in the middle of the park. Off to the side was a temporary stage with a dozen elves lined up, wearing crisp, forest-green uniforms and pointed leather hats. The carriage stopped right before the stage and one of the elves came running up and held his hand out. "Ms. Calhoun, we are so happy you made it."

"Uhh…thanks?" I shot Pyper a confused look, but placed my hand in the elf's and let him help me out of the carriage. He was tall and thin, with shimmering green eyes and angular bone structure. Handsome, in an intriguing sort of way.

"This way, please. Then we can get the ceremony started." He tugged me up the stairs to the stage as the other elves broke into song, singing, "Do You Hear What I Hear."

Their voices were as sweet as angels', sending chills over my skin. I was completely mesmerized by their infectious tone.

"Have a seat." The elf's charming smile reached his eyes.

I glanced around him at the high-backed wooden chair.

Then I turned and spotted Pyper waving her fingers at me while she moved toward the tree.

"Um, why?" I asked, confused.

"You're the leader of the New Orleans coven, are you not?"

"Yes, but—"

"You are our honored guest." He bowed and waved his hand with a flourish. "Our Christmas queen."

Sitting on some fancy throne, watching the festivities was the last thing I wanted to do. I'd rather be hanging out with Pyper, wandering around, being awed by the grandeur until we were too frozen to do anything but run back home and wrap ourselves in fuzzy blankets on the couch.

But the way the elves were all gathered around looking at me expectantly, I felt I didn't have a choice and reluctantly shuffled to the chair. At least it was sort of flattering to be asked to play the Christmas queen.

As soon as my butt hit the chair, the elves ceased singing and closed ranks around me. An invisible force brushed up against me, and the pressure increased, crushing me as if I'd been stuffed in a vise. I opened my mouth to cry out, but the air rushed out of my lungs along with all the joy from the carriage ride through the French Quarter.

My eyes watered and I lurched forward, sliding out of the chair. The elves formed a solid barrier, completely concealing me from the activities in the square.

"Our apologies, Ms. Calhoun," the elf who'd helped me out of the carriage said into my ear. "We regret the circumstances, but they can't be helped."

"Circumstances?" I gasped out. "You're stealing my energy."

"Only because we have to."

I glanced back, glaring at the elf and reached for the magic pulsing in my chest. But it slipped from my mental grasp and the harder I tried to grab hold, the more elusive it became. I let out a huff of frustration and crawled up on my knees.

The elves seemed to grow, towering over me.

One of the elves started singing again, her sweet voice belting out a heart-rending version of "Silent Night."

"Why are you doing this?" I said through clenched teeth, trying to block out the pulsing ache running through my entire body.

The elf turned slowly and stared down at me. His apologetic expression vanished, replaced by determined eyes and hardened features as his body vibrated with tension. "Freedom."

CHAPTER 3

"*E*xcuse me?" I shot back, but the tall elf had already moved to center stage in front of the rest of his group. They all joined the angelic elf in her version of "Silent Night." From what I could see of the crowd, the elves had captivated their attention and everything else had stopped—including the Twelve Days of Christmas parade.

The chatter vanished, and every last soul was completely captivated. Including me. There was a bittersweet sadness to the song that was stirring emotions deep in my gut. And the more they sang, the more my heart swelled to nearly bursting.

I shook my head, trying to snap out of whatever was happening. It was a spell. It had to be. Their voices were too intoxicating.

Using the chair, I clawed my way up until I was finally standing on my own two feet. But they were cemented to the stage, making it impossible to move.

Holy hell. I needed to do something, anything, before the crazy elves drained the last of my energy. I lifted my arm, struggling against the invisible pressure, and reached forward. If I could just touch one of them, I could tap into my magic and take back what they'd stolen from me. But just before I grabbed the shoulder of the nearest elf, a female with gorgeous porcelain skin and big blue eyes, she spun and hissed at me through ugly pointed teeth. Her hands morphed into boney claws, complete with sharpened, blood-red nails.

I jerked back and instinctively shot a bolt of my white magic at her. She held her hand up, connecting with my magic, but it just turned her hand back to normal flesh with snowflake-decorated nails.

My magic hadn't affected her at all. In fact, judging by the pleased smile she sent me, it appeared she welcomed it. "Thank you," she said, her body starting to shimmer with a coating of my magic. "Every little bit helps."

Whoa. I'd sent a bolt of magic intending to incapacitate her, or at least zap her enough to make her back off. But it appeared she'd embraced it and used the magic to heighten her own power. I scowled. "Helps what? What do you want from me?"

"Relax, witch," the elf said. "It's not our intention to harm anyone. Not if we can help it anyway."

"Not if you can help it?" I echoed, but the elf had already turned and joined the others in their song.

Their voices rose above the crowd in the square, and suddenly the pressure lifted and my limbs were light. I had the strange sense that if I had wings I could fly.

The elves jumped from the stage and scattered, each of them doing back flips and cartwheels into the crowd. Half of them stopped and kneeled on their hands and knees. The other half ran across the square, leaped off their fellow elves and spun in the air, putting on one hell of an acrobatic show. The crowd clapped and hooted their approval.

"What in the world?" I glanced around in utter confusion. Had that all been about stealing my energy for their performance? But what had she meant when she said they didn't want to harm anyone if they could help it? The other one had said they wanted freedom. Were they under someone's control? And what about the demonic appearance of the elf before she'd absorbed my magic? That wasn't innocent.

Crap on toast. Where were Bea and my coven when I needed them? I whipped out my phone and hit the on button.

Nothing.

I pressed harder.

Nothing.

"Dammit!" The phone was dead. It had been fully charged earlier in the evening. Whatever the elves had done to me, the magic had affected my phone, as well.

"Jade!" Pyper stood in front of the stage. "Get down here."

Relief washed through me, and I ran down the stairs to her side. Clutching her arm, I asked, "Are you okay?"

"Sure." She handed me a mug with a candy cane garnish. "Why wouldn't I be?"

I frowned and pulled her away from the stage. I glanced back at the innocuous structure and stifled a shiver. "Something is seriously off with those elves."

Her eyebrows shot up as she sipped her drink. "Aren't all circus-performer type people a little 'off?'"

"Not like this." I glanced around and lowered my voice not wanting to attract any attention. "I think they might be demons."

Her eyes widened as she clutched my arm. "You're serious?"

I nodded. Demons could take on any form. And hadn't she said Kane had already gone after a demon in Santa clothing? But they weren't exactly acting like demons. They'd left me unharmed after they'd presumably gotten what they wanted. And they hadn't been nearly destructive enough. At least not yet.

Pyper turned and eyed the elves dancing through the Twelve Days of Christmas parade. Then she cocked her head to the side and frowned in concentration.

"What?"

"They aren't demons." Her brow wrinkled. "The message is unclear, but I think I'm hearing they are lost souls."

"Is a ghost talking to you?"

"Not one. More like a dozen." She grimaced. "They are chattering over each other and fading in and out. It's hard to get a clear connection." Shaking her head, she clenched her fists and gave me a pained look. "Sorry. They're gone. Vanished."

"All of them?" I asked.

"Yeah." She turned to stare at the elves again. "They were scared, Jade. Whatever they are, it's not right."

More spectators started to fill the square. It was getting harder and harder to spot the elves. "We have to call Bea and the coven."

She nodded, her expression still troubled.

"Pyper?"

"Huh?"

I held up my phone. "It's dead."

"Oh." She dug into her pocket and handed me her phone.

I pressed the on button and let out a frustrated sigh when nothing happened. "Yours is dead, too."

She didn't acknowledge my response. She was too busy staring at the elves. They'd moved on from their acrobatics to partnering with the nine ladies dancing from the parade.

The remaining three elves were standing on a raised platform in front of the tree, singing "White Christmas." They were using microphones and had captivated the crowd again. Pyper started to move toward them, and that's when I saw it.

Silver light coated everyone in the crowd, and the elves were siphoning it off one note at a time. Through their singing, the elves had somehow tapped into the auras of the spectators and were stealing faint traces of their spirit.

"No!" I cried and lurched forward, but no one paid any attention to me.

My chest tightened as panic set in. Spirit was a person's life force. If the elves took enough, we'd end up with a massacre. A real nightmare before Christmas.

"Pyper!" I called, but she was already disappearing into the mass of people, all of whom were clearly under the elves' spell.

Christ. I couldn't magic my way out of this one. Not on my own. I needed help and fast.

I had two choices: run home and use my landline, or shadow walk. One of my abilities was to enter the shadow world and reenter this world at another point. The shadows were the world between this one and Hell, where souls roamed who were not destined for either the angel realm or Hell. Only lately, the demons had been stealing those souls for only God knew what. It was one of my jobs to rescue them from such a fate.

Unfortunately, I wasn't as good at walking the shadows as Kane was. He could've walked us straight to Bea's house. I could get myself to his club, because I knew there was a portal there, but anything else would be iffy. The club it was. I'd call Bea and Lucien, my second in command of the coven, as soon as I got there.

Taking a deep breath, I concentrated on Kane's club and took a step, willing myself into the shadows.

The world turned to shades of gray and the people in the square shimmered silver. Everyone except the elves.

They were dark shadows, and all of them were decrepit versions of themselves in the form of stone statues.

Horror swept through me, and tears filled my eyes as I realized exactly what they were. They were from Hell, but they weren't demons.

They were trapped souls.

CHAPTER 4

*I*n Hell, souls were trapped in stone statues. Somehow, the elves in the square had found a way to manifest in our world. But standing in the shadow world, I could see the dark bindings of Hell tethered to each of them. Their trip to the streets of New Orleans would be short-lived.

Unless… Freedom. That's what the elf had said they were after.

And they were going to do it by stealing the spirits of the innocents in the square.

Crap!

No time to mess around. I took another step and concentrated on the club.

I instantly popped into the middle of the strip club, seemingly out of nowhere. A man leaning forward in a blue-velvet chair jerked back, obviously startled. Then he let his gaze travel down my body, taking in my skimpy Mrs. Claus outfit.

"Well, hello there, sweetheart. How much for a lap dance?"

I tugged the teal coat closed and scowled at him while Lady Gaga sang something about her Christmas tree being delicious.

"Hey!" the guy called after me, as I strode off toward the office.

"Jade?" Charlie, the club manager, called after me.

I paused at the office door, waiting for her to catch up.

"I thought you and Kane had a special night planned?" She also did a quick perusal of my outfit and gave me an approving smile as she nodded. "I bet that heated things up."

"That would've been nice. Instead he's fighting a Santa demon and I've got a dozen elves trying to crawl their way out of Hell as we speak." My heels clattered on the hardwood as I hurried over to the desk.

Charlie shut the door behind her and stared at me, her eyes wide. "Elves?"

I waved a hand as I picked up the phone. "Trapped souls dressed up as elves. Don't ask."

"That's…different."

"You're telling me." Charlie was no stranger to the paranormal happenings we dealt with on a daily basis, but even I had to admit dealing with rogue elves and Santa demons was way out of our norm.

"Merry Christmas!" Bea's voice rang on the other end of the line.

"I hate to do this to you, but we have a problem."

"Jade? What's wrong?"

"I need you and anyone else you can rustle up to meet me down at Jackson Square. I have a dozen elves trying to escape from Hell."

"Demons?" Her tone was serious now and I heard the squeak of a door opening on her end.

"No. If that was the case I'd know what to do. Or at least who to call. These are trapped souls, and it looks like they're using the spirit of the crowd to somehow free themselves."

There was dead silence on the other end of the line.

"Bea?"

"Trapped souls," she said by way of answer. "Son of a goddess's whore. This is not good."

I raised my eyebrows in Charlie's direction. It was unusual for Bea to swear, not that she'd said anything too outrageous. I just wasn't used to it.

Charlie mouthed, "What?"

I shook my head. "No, it isn't. And worse, they seem to be able to feed off my power. I'm not sure what to do."

"We need the coven. Lucien and Rosalee are here. We'll round up as many of the others as we can."

"Okay. Thanks. And hurry would you? Pyper's under their spell."

Bea let out a frustrated grunt. "Got it. I'll be there in less than five minutes."

"Thanks."

"Meet me at the front gate." She took a deep breath. "And Jade?"

"Yeah?"

"Whatever you do, don't use any more magic until we get there."

I hadn't planned on it, but if I was attacked, I wasn't sure what else I could do. "All right."

"Five minutes," she said again, and the call went dead.

I put the phone down and pressed my palms against the shiny desk top as I glanced at the wall clock. Four minutes, forty seconds. I didn't want to leave just yet, because without Bea and the rest of the coven, I was useless. "Now what?" I muttered to myself.

"Isn't Bea coming?" Charlie asked, clearly having picked up on at least part of my conversation.

"Oh, yes. But I can't use magic until I have back-up. So far, nothing I've tried has worked. They just end up stealing it."

"Well, that means there's only one thing to do," Charlie said.

"What's that?"

"Take this." She opened a filing cabinet and pulled out a small satchel. "Everything you need to fight evil is in here."

I gave her an odd look. Charlie didn't have magic. Her talents were in managing the club so Kane didn't have to.

She smiled. "It's an emergency stash."

I took it and peeked inside. There were a couple vials of potions. One was a blinding potion, somewhat similar to pepper spray, and the other was a freezing potion. Defensive stuff. Along with the potions there were a couple of herb bundles and a small dagger with a jewel-encrusted hilt. It wasn't a demon-hunting dagger. It was too small for that, but there was magic pulsing in those stones. Protective magic. "Where did you get this?"

"Bea. She said they're already spelled, so even those of us not blessed with magic could use them in an emergency. It's a mundane's survival kit for those of us caught in the crosshairs."

I shook my head, marveling at Bea's thoughtfulness. Putting my friends in danger was always one of my biggest fears. The items in the satchel weren't going to stop a demon on the loose, but they could slow one down long enough for someone to get the heck out of dodge. I wasn't sure what any of the items could do for me back at Jackson Square, but at this point anything was welcome.

"Thanks." I hugged Charlie. "Put the word out to stay away from the Square, would you? If anyone makes noise about heading that direction, steer them elsewhere for now."

"Will do, Jade." She gave me a small smile. "And you be safe, all right? I expect to see your gorgeous face tomorrow for Christmas dinner. And if you're laid up recovering... again, and I have to suffer through another night of Lailah and Lucien arguing about the state of the witch community, you're going to pay. I'll make you suffer. Got it?"

I chuckled, remembering her horrified expression on Thanksgiving after the pair had gotten into an hour-long, technical debate about the magical properties of the incredibly phallic-looking clam, the geoduck. It turns out, there are some rumors it's the next big thing in treating erectile dysfunction for magical beings. Lailah and her significant other, Jonathon, had been a part of the initial testing.

I grimaced, remembering her tale of Jonathon suddenly being unable to stop himself from making out with an actual troll. A small gray one with yellow teeth. A shudder ran through me. "I hear you. No one wants to suffer that fate."

"Good." Charlie smiled, the humor reaching her pale green eyes. "Because it's all about me and my needs."

"Obviously," I said, laughing, and then I sobered. "Seriously, if you see Kane, we could use him and any of the other demon hunters. I'm not sure exactly what is going on, but it's not good."

"I'm on it." Charlie put her arm around my waist. "Let me walk you out so no other customers get any bright ideas."

"Thanks," I said gratefully, not blaming the man who'd asked for a lap dance. I had dressed to elicit that very reaction, albeit, from my husband.

Charlie escorted me back into the middle of the club, near the invisible portal. Then as nonchalantly as I could, knowing Charlie would brush off any awkward questions if anyone noticed, I stepped back into the shadows and right back into Jackson Square.

And reappeared sitting on Santa's lap.

CHAPTER 5

"Whoa!" I jumped up, intending to scramble off Santa's lap, but the man's—no demon's—arm wrapped around my waist, pulling me back. He wore the traditional Santa suit, except for his hat. It was black velvet. He was Evil Santa.

"Well, well, well," he said, in a ho, ho, ho tone. "What do we have here?"

"Let go," I ordered, my body coiled, ready to strike.

"I don't think so." He waved a hand at the crowd. "They're waiting for the show to start."

It was then I noticed I was back on the stage, both of us sitting in the Christmas queen's chair. And right in the front row of the audience were the dozen elves, each of them kneeling on one knee as they scowled at us.

"It's ingenious, isn't it?" he asked conversationally.

"What is?" A small twinge of magic stirred in my chest. If I used it on him, would it work? Or would he be able to absorb it just as the elf had? I had to pick my moment carefully and be ready for both scenarios, otherwise this could end very badly for me. I couldn't outmuscle the demon. His strong grip meant he could take me straight to Hell if he wanted to. Getting free was priority number one.

"The way they managed to harness the magic pulsing through the Quarter in order to rise. And then they tapped you and the rest of these *parasites* to steal your energy... It's a thing of beauty. History in the making. Really impressive."

"Parasites?" There was no hiding the disdain in my tone. If anything demons were the parasites. They got their power from human souls.

He laughed evilly, his talons pressing into my skin, a not-so-subtle threat that he'd have no problem slicing me to shreds if he decided I was no longer of use. "Careful, white witch. Or when I send those elves straight back to Hell, you'll be first in line."

The hell I would. But right then was not the time to argue. I was too busy watching Pyper inch toward the stage. What was she up to? I wanted to shout, to tell her to stay away. Or to send her back to the house to wait for us, but I couldn't without drawing the demon's attention to her. She wouldn't anyway. Her loyalty was unwavering.

The demon was too distracted to notice her making her way onto the stage, though. He was eyeballing the souls trying to escape Hell. He raised his hand and pointed at the tall skinny one right in the middle. And once the elf was staring right at him, Santa demon slowly curled his hand into a fist.

The elf's eyes bulged and the illusion of his flesh stripped away, leaving only the decrepit, decayed skeleton of a lost soul.

Horrified anger exploded in my chest. Suffering in Hell until the end of time as the demons fed off him was the worst fate anyone could suffer. No one deserved that. Not even the worst among us.

Not trusting my magic, I defaulted to self-defense mode. While the demon was busy torturing the elf, I jerked my arm up, and with every bit of force I could muster, I jammed my elbow into the crook of the demon's arm.

He grunted, more in surprise than pain, but it was enough to break his hold on me. I jumped to my feet and spun, facing him. Magic tingled at my fingertips. I could still feel the echo of his talons on my bare skin, and the desire to blast him with everything I had consumed me. And as the demon lurched forward, I brought one hand up and unleashed a torrent of destruction on him, hitting him squarely in the eyes.

He let out a loud roar, but kept coming for me.

"Now!" I yelled.

Pyper rose up from behind him, the potion from the satchel in her hand, and as I stepped aside, she doused the demon.

He froze, his hand just inches from closing around my neck.

I stood there, my eyes narrowed as I scowled at the Santa demon.

"Jade," Pyper said, grabbing my hand. "Let's get out of here."

"I can't." My gaze cut to the elves, now scrambling back away from the stage. With the demon temporarily immobilized, they were freed from his hold. "When this spell wears off, all these people will be in danger."

She let out a frustrated huff. "Well, where the hell are Kane and the rest of the Brotherhood? Aren't they supposed to be fighting demons?"

I shook my head. "I don't know. Maybe we're in a dead zone, and they can't detect anything?" The only reasons Kane and the other hunters wouldn't have shown up were if the demon didn't register on their radar, or if all of them already had their hands full. Dammit. Why hadn't I thought to try to get in touch with Kane while I was at the club?

Because Pyper had said he was already fighting a demon, and I hadn't known we'd have one of our own. That's why.

Crap.

"Oh, thank God," Pyper said, pointing toward the entrance of Jackson Square.

I couldn't help the surprised laugh that came bubbling out and quickly turned to hilarity as I shook from the ridiculousness of it all.

Bea, the former coven leader of New Orleans, was wearing a red sequined ball gown and standing up on a carriage, her legs spread apart for balance with the reigns in her hands. Auburn hair flew out behind her while half my coven followed, riding adult-sized tricycles. And that wasn't even the most ridiculous part. Her two "horses" were really jackasses wearing antlers and red noses.

"Who knew Rudolph was in town?" Pyper said with a snicker.

"And what's with the three-wheelers?" I added. Lucien and Rosalee were right behind Bea, both of them also wearing sequined formal ware.

"What the hell is Lucien wearing?" Pyper grimaced. "Good Lord. That should be illegal."

His sports coat was bright emerald green, all sequins with a tie to match. I had half a mind to spell him into another outfit.

"Looks like we interrupted a...party?" I turned to her my eyebrows lifted.

She shook her head. "I dunno, but by the looks of it, I'm glad I wasn't invited."

I chuckled and started to move forward to meet Bea. But just as I took my second step, a loud roar of frustration came from behind me, drowning out all the noise from the crowd.

The demon. Shit. I'd been so busy eyeing Bea and the coven that I'd all but forgotten he was back there.

I spun, ready to spell him again, but he was too quick. Too pissed.

He pounced. Both hands went for my throat, and as I grabbed hold of my magic, the large demon squeezed, cutting off my air.

Jesus! My magic dissipated and instantly I was rendered useless. My air had been cut off and I was already going lightheaded.

"Hey, asshole!" I heard Pyper cry.

He ignored her.

"I have something you want." Her voice was far away now, as if she'd left the stage.

The demon only pressed harder. My vision started to turn black.

Panic set in. Magic pulsed in my chest. Magic I couldn't control. Not while I was on the verge of passing out. A burst of energy shot forth from me, and the demon released me, screaming as he flew across the stage.

Pyper stood off to the side, holding the empty potion bottle. I started to move toward her, but she put her hand up. "Wait!"

Then she pointed to the stage and the pool of liquid. The freezing potion was seeping toward me. She'd been trying to spell him again and missed when I tossed the demon. "Thanks. Between the two of us, he didn't have a chance."

She opened her mouth to speak, but the demon came up behind her and wrapped an ugly pock-marked arm around her throat.

Gross. My spell must've broken his human illusion. Now he was gray, with wrinkly, leather-like skin, electric-yellow eyes, and a skeletal body cloaked in an oversized Santa suit.

"Step off her, demon," I said, magic crackling at my fingertips.

"I don't think so." He snarled and lowered his head toward her neck.

I screamed, certain he was going to bite her, but he only took a big whiff. Holy crow. Was this some sort of demon fetish? But then I noticed Pyper wilting and the light dimming in her eyes while his illusion snapped back into place.

"No!" I cried and gritted my teeth. There was no way to blast him without hitting Pyper first. I dove, barely missing the potion still pooled on the stage, and grabbed the satchel. In one desperate movement, I came up with the small dagger in my hand. I felt its magic pulsing in my palm and knew if I could get it anywhere near his heart, this would all be over.

But he turned, keeping Pyper in front of him.

There was a commotion of heavy footsteps behind me, followed by shouts of panic and Bea ordering the coven members to hold their ground. I glanced out of the corner of my eye, and sucked in a hard breath. There were another dozen Santas facing off with the coven members.

Demons. Every last one of them.

"Back off, witch," the demon in front of me ordered. "Or I'll kill her right now."

Pyper clawed at his arm and threw her head back, aiming for his nose. Bullseye. The demon stumbled, shaking his head. I didn't waste any time. Jumping over the freezing potion, I skirted around them and slammed the dagger into Santa demon's back.

He stiffened, and then snarled as he tried to spin. Pyper hooked her foot around his, turned and kneed him in the groin. His eyes widened with surprised as he fell to the side, more from being knocked off balance than from any obvious pain.

"Pyper!" I reached out, trying to grab her as they both went down in slow motion right into the freezing potion.

Dammit. If only she'd been able to loosen his hold on her, that move would've been perfect. It was still impressive, though. Who else had the cajones to knee a demon in the balls?

The two lay sprawled on the stage while the remaining Santa demons battled with my coven members. Spells and bolts of white and black magic whizzed through the air. The giant Christmas tree was on fire. The twelve days of Christmas participants had vanished, and the only people left were the elves. They were busy lobbing what looked to be little sugar-plum bombs at the demons.

Total mayhem.

I had to do something. But first, I needed to get Pyper from the asshat Santa. He was lying partially on top of her, his large frame, pinning her down. Another blast of anger shot through me, and as I reached down to grab her hand, I gave the demon a swift kick in the ribs. He flipped over and landed with a thud on the stage.

I quickly pulled Pyper over to the edge, and just as I was

about to reverse the freezing spell, a shimmering light crawled over Santa until it encased his entire body.

Oh, goddess. What now? I zapped Pyper and muttered, "*Revive.*"

Her eyes flew open as she sucked in a gasp of air.

"Let's go," I said, my instincts telling me we had to get as far away from the demon as possible.

She wobbled, but clutched my hand and managed to keep up.

We were only a few feet from the stage when the light around the Santa demon turned ice blue and then burst into flames. He flailed his limbs, and his face contorted with silent screams as the fire consumed him, shot straight up in the air and winked out, leaving nothing but black ash on the stage.

"Holy shit," Pyper said.

"I think maybe Santa's naughty list just got a little shorter." I stared at the pile of ash, trying to figure out what had happened.

"Cute," Pyper said with a heavy dose of sarcasm. "But now might not—"

"Jade!" Kane's voice permeated my haze of confusion.

I spun, finding him and a stream of demon hunters sprinting into the square. He was wearing his dress pants and the button down shirt I'd gotten him a few weeks ago. The one I'd told him I was looking forward to ripping off of him the next chance I got. He'd clearly been dressed up for our romantic ride through the Quarter before he'd been called to battle demons.

A pang of regret stabbed me, and I glanced down at my Mrs. Claus outfit. My skirt was ripped, and the fake white fur was smudged with dirt. So much for being a sexy little Christmas present.

Kane came to a stop right in front of me, his dagger out, as another one of the other Santa demons finally spotted us. The demon hissed, and Kane threw his dagger, hitting the demon right in the eye. The demon recoiled and then suddenly vanished. Kane's dagger fell to the ground, the stone in the handle gleaming with magical light. He flicked his wrist and the dagger zoomed back into his hand.

He glanced around, noted his fellow brothers and the coven expertly taking out the remaining demons and then turned to me, unconcerned. "What's going on?"

I raised both eyebrows. "You don't know?"

He shook his head. "No. One minute we were tracking these Santa demons in Uptown, and then the next they disappeared. We followed, but when we got here, it appeared the square was empty and it was as if there was an invisible wall keeping us out. Something just changed. A spell was neutralized or something and then we were able to charge in."

"I think I know what happened." Pulling him over to the front of the stage, I pointed at the black ash. "We destroyed that demon. Right after that you guys showed up."

Kane cursed. "Was he wearing a black Santa hat?"

"Yes? Did you have a run-in with him?"

"Yeah. He was Kyros Kringle."

My eyes went wide. "As in related to Kris Kringle?"

"Yes." His brow furrowed. "Santa, the real one, is an ancient witch. His brother was an angel and fell centuries ago. I learned tonight that Kyros periodically surfaces on Christmas Eve to try to bait his brother."

"Uh, Santa's real?" I asked.

"Jade. Focus." Kane peered at the stage. "How did you do this?"

"I can't believe Santa's real and I killed his demon brother," I muttered to myself, watching as Bea single-handedly opened a portal to Hell and sent back two fake Santas.

"Jade." Kane snapped his fingers.

"Yeah?"

"What did you do to Kyros?"

"Oh. We used the dagger and the freezing potion in the emergency kit you and Bea left with Charlie. I think it was the dagger that did it in the end."

He jumped up on the stage, poked through the ash and found the dagger. Then he nodded. "Yeah. This is what did it. Only you didn't end the demon; just shed his human form and sent him back to Hell."

"Dammit," Pyper said, straightening her smudged silver dress. I wasn't the only one with dirt stains ruining my outfit.

I wasn't sure if she was upset about her dress or the demon.

Kane grabbed the small dagger, leaped from the stage and helped his demon-hunter brothers finish off the last of the demons.

When the last one was finally gone, Bea closed the portal, climbed back into her jackass drawn carriage, and collapsed in the seat.

I touched Kane's arm. "I'll be right back."

He gave me a kiss on the temple. "Sure, love. I need to talk to the Brotherhood anyway."

Pyper fell into step beside me, and the pair of us jogged over to Bea. Unlike our clothes, her red sequined dress was in perfect order. How did she always manage to battle evil and still look like she'd just walked out of a salon?

Except this time, she had her eyes closed and the back of her hand draped over her forehead.

"Bea?"

She jerked and sat straight up. "Oh, hello, ladies. I was just resting my eyes while I try to come up with a plan to free those elves."

I turned and eyed the group of Hell-bound souls. Most of them were gathered around the burnt Christmas tree holding hands. Their heads were bowed as if in prayer. There was a sad air about them that made my chest tighten. They weren't giving up were they? Lailah had helped us free souls from Hell before, though not ones that were already trapped in stone. "Is there something we can do together? Or call Lailah maybe?"

"No, as much as Lailah would like to help, this isn't something that she can do safely. It isn't something any of us can do safely. There are only two ways to free them: go to Hell and magically break the binding on their tombs, or take the life energy of magical beings to give them the strength to do it themselves. Unfortunately, the amount of energy the elves need makes it entirely too dangerous, due to how long they've been trapped down there. If we tried it, someone could be seriously injured, or even killed."

A shiver ran through me. Hadn't they been siphoning my life force earlier? If given the chance would they have drained me to save themselves?

"I don't think they are really elves," Pyper said.

"Tell that to him," the lead elf said, now standing beside Bea pointing to the sky.

And just above us was a twinkling sleigh, lit up in bright

white lights with a team of… Was that reindeer? No. I blinked.

"Whoa," Pyper said.

Bea grinned.

I stared opened-mouthed at the spectacle barreling right for us. "Santa?"

CHAPTER 6

"*H*o, ho, ho!" Santa called out, just like one would expect him to. The sleigh, powered by nine reindeer, landed just in front of the charred Christmas tree. "Merry Christmas!"

"You've got to be kidding me," Pyper muttered.

"What, you're not wowed by Santa?" I asked her, wondering if we'd slipped into some sort of alternate reality.

Her blue eyes flashed with irritation. "Where was he when his brother was trying to kill us?"

"Good question."

The dozen elves kneeled in front of Santa, their heads bowed and hands clasped in front of them.

The jolly man in the sleigh glanced around the square, frowned, and then jumped down, his black boots hitting the cement walk with a thud. "What's going on?" Suspicion replaced his practiced cheer. "Where's Kyros?"

"I sent his ass back to Hell." I placed my hands on my hips and narrowed my eyes at him. Just because he was Santa didn't mean he was trustworthy. "Why? Were you here to join him in his…ah, activities?"

Santa turned to me, intelligence and patience radiating off him. "Ms. Calhoun." He smiled. "It's a pleasure to finally meet you." His gaze traveled the length of my body. A faint trace of distaste brushed up against my skin. "Isn't that an interesting take on Jessica's uniform?"

Heat burned my cheeks. Mrs. Claus's first name was Jessica. I pulled the teal jacket closed and ignored the remark. Awkward.

"Kris," Bea said. "It's nice to see you again."

Kane reappeared by my side and it was then I noticed the Brotherhood had already vanished. The demons were gone. Their job was done.

"Bea. You're a vision as always. And still kicking demon ass. Don't think I didn't see you flying in here, your magic blazing. Impressive."

I let out the breath I hadn't realized I'd been holding.

Kane wrapped his arm around me, let his gaze sweep over my body, and whispered, "Interesting indeed. I assume it was part of my present?"

I nodded, a whole new kind of heat making me flush.

"Then I can't wait to unwrap you as soon as we get home."

A smile tugged at my lips, and I no longer cared what Santa thought. Finally Christmas was shaping up to be something magical.

Bea slipped her arm through Santa's and tugged him toward the elves. "Thanks. You flatter me, but right now we have more pressing matters.

My coven closed in around us, their collective apprehension making my skin itch. They didn't trust the elves or Santa. Couldn't say I blamed them. Santa was way too cavalier, and the elves were loose cannons. They'd already put me and Pyper in danger. What else would they do?

"These souls are still tied to Hell," I said. "Be careful. They tried to steal my life energy in order to free themselves."

His eyes narrowed as he took a step forward toward the leader. Then he turned chalk-white as he kneeled down right in front of him. "Nico?"

The elf lifted his head, tears standing in his dark eyes. "Mr. Kringle. We never wanted to hurt anyone. I swear. We just…"

"Oh, Nico." Santa put his hand on the elf's shoulder and glanced around at the other elves who were all now staring at him with a mixture of hope and…was that shame?

"I think you might know these souls," Bea said to Santa, her tone gentle.

Santa nodded slowly. "They used to work for me." He swallowed. "A long time ago."

"They really are elves?" Pyper said, her voice carrying over the square.

"We were," Nico said, still staring at Santa.

Santa stood and took a step back.

Bea placed her hand on his arm. "Don't you think they've suffered enough, Kris?"

He turned to her, his eyes wide with surprise. "You know what happened?"

"I heard the rumors." She gave him a gentle smile. "You could give them a second chance, you know. Because Kyros bound them, and the two of you share DNA, only your magic can free them, though you'll likely need an extra boost. I'm sure Jade and the coven would lend you their power. If you asked them."

"Second chance? Not if they're going to suck the energy of my witches," I said. Then I cringed. Santa, and apparently his elves, needed help. Was I the Scrooge here?

Santa jerked and then stood tall as he faced me. "Ms. Calhoun, no elf of mine will intentionally harm anyone ever again. It is with my deepest sincerity that I must apologize for the way my elves have behaved. I assure you it is not acceptable."

One of the elves let out a tiny sob.

"Enough, Tinnie," Santa said sharply to the female elf. "You all have a lot to atone for, but I do not believe your crime is so severe that you deserve to suffer in Hell for the rest of eternity. If I request the help of this coven, will you all agree to a code of conduct spell that will also bind you to the North Pole for the next ten years?"

"Ten years confinement?" I asked, aghast. I wasn't too pleased with the elves, but Hell was a place that could break even the strongest will. Punishing them further was going overboard wasn't it? "Isn't that a little harsh? I mean, haven't they already suffered enough?"

"You're a kind soul, Ms. Calhoun." Santa smiled at me. "I'm not talking about incarceration, if that's what you're thinking. Only that they'll be contracted to work for me."

"For free?" Pyper said, just as skeptical as I was.

He chuckled. "No. They will be paid on par with the rest of my elves. But considering the circumstances, I think they'll need a readjustment period. I think it's best if that happens in a safe environment. Then after their term is up, they can decide if they want to acclimate into the modern world."

I turned to Bea. "I'm not sure I completely understand."

"Give us just a moment, will you, Kris?" Bea said and then pulled me back over toward the stage. "Listen, Jade. The elves have been in Hell for a few centuries."

My stomach dropped. "Centuries?"

She nodded. "Yes. And from what I understand, this particular group made a deal with Kyros in order to...ah, become more human-like."

I pursed my lips. Other than their outfits, they seemed plenty human to me. "I still don't understand."

"You will once the spell is done. Anyway, they were desperate to change their circumstances. The world was different back then. They couldn't just leave the North Pole and integrate into normal society. They were too different. There was zero chance they'd be accepted. Kris wouldn't let them go because he was afraid for their safety, and the spells to modify their appearance were too rudimentary. There are safer, more advanced spells now that could help them change their appearance if they choose to, though that isn't necessary. Elves live among us. Not many, because from what I understand, the North Pole truly is a magical place. But these twelve? They wanted something different. And they were desperate for it."

"They made a deal with a demon didn't they?" There was no other explanation. They'd sold their souls.

"Yes," she whispered, eyeing the elves still kneeling before Santa. "They didn't understand the ramifications and once the papers were signed..." She let out a sigh. "Well, they did get their human appearances, but they also got a nice long stay in Hell. The fine print indentured them for a millennium. A millennium, Jade. Can you imagine?"

A lump got caught in my throat. They'd just wanted to

live a normal existence like the rest of us, but instead, they'd ended up living a nightmare. "I'll do it."

She sent me a grateful smile. "I honestly don't think they meant to harm anyone. People do desperate things when they feel like they have no choices."

"I get that." And I really did. Not to mention the thought of not helping them made my stomach turn. "Okay, everyone. I'd like to lend our magic to Old Saint Nick here so he can free the elves from Hell. Who's with me?"

Every last member of my coven nodded or called, "Me!"

Bea grinned at them. "Thank you. It would work best if we form a circle around Kris and the elves."

I took the northern most spot on our makeshift circle, while Lucien stood across from me, and Bea stood to the right. Kane and Pyper stood near the jackass-drawn carriage.

And right in the middle of the circle was Santa, with his elves gathered around him.

"Ready?" I asked Lucien.

He nodded.

Without hesitation, I held my arms straight up in the air and called, *"Circumda."*

A brilliant stream of magic crackled to life, pulsing through each of the coven members as we joined hands.

Santa tilted his head up, breathing in through his nose. Then he turned to me. "Well done, Ms. Calhoun. Thank you."

I opened my mouth to answer, but before I could get the words out, Santa raised his own arms, seemed to grow to almost twice his size, and in a voice that boomed over the square, he said, "Elves of the darkest night, return to thy sights. Embrace the joys, laughter, and flights. From now until forevermore, may each of my charges be wards of the Northern Lights."

We all waited expectantly.

Absolutely nothing happened.

I glanced at Bea. She gave me a one armed shrug as if to say she had no idea.

The combined magic of the coven still pulsed through us, more powerful than ever, and I started to wonder if Santa had tapped into it at all.

I cleared my throat. "Uh, Santa? Are you sure—"

"Shh, Ms. Calhoun," he said so softly, I barely heard him. "It's coming."

What was coming? I frantically scanned the square, afraid of what he might have called. But still I saw nothing. Squinting up toward the dark sky, I let out an audible gasp.

"Snow?" Pyper said from behind me. "Oh, man," she whined. "I'm going to freeze in this dress."

So was I. But it was too magical for me to care. It filled the sky, floating down in soft, fluffy flakes. It wasn't unheard of for it to snow in New Orleans. It did happen on rare occasions, but not when it was fifty eight degrees outside.

"It's gorgeous," I said as the first flakes hit the top of the burnt tree. The limbs started to turn white with the layer of snow. But then the snow started to sparkle and melted off, leaving behind restored, green limbs. I let out a delighted gasp and covered my mouth as the first flakes landed on the elves.

"It's working." Bea's face lit up into a huge grin.

I followed her gaze and blinked.

Holy crap on a pogo stick.

The very human-looking elves were morphing into slightly shorter, rounder versions of themselves with big round eyes, longer fingers, and weathered skin.

The female elf took one look at Nico and started to cry.

Through her tears she laughed and danced around until she came face to face with Santa. "Thank you, Mr. Kringle. Thank you!" She threw her arms around him, hugging him fiercely.

Santa returned her hug and laughed with her, his jolly sound creating a chain reaction through the newly freed elves.

"It worked," Nico said staring down at his newly shaped hands. "I can't believe it. We're free."

"Congratulations," Bea said, smiling.

Kane stepped up beside me, his demeanor sober. "Yes, and there's no doubt it created a great disruption within the demon realm. It's best if you all go now."

"He's right," Bea agreed.

"Into the sleigh," Santa ordered. "All of you!"

The elves wasted no time. And even though I would've sworn the sleigh was only big enough for two people, all twelve of them piled in without trouble.

Huh. All that extra room must've been how Santa transported all those packages.

"We're off," Santa called, as they lifted off the ground. "Thank you, everyone. Merry Christmas. And to all a good night."

We all waved and a second later the sleigh vanished into the steady stream of snow now blanketing the streets of New Orleans.

"Well, that was...something," Pyper said, as the coven members broke out into a snowball fight.

"Something?" I echoed as I took in the lush tree all lit up with twinkle lights. "Looks like a miracle to me."

"That it is, Jade," Bea said, as she climbed back into her jackass-drawn carriage. "Anyone need a ride? I have a party to get back to."

Kane and I glanced at each other, both of us shaking our heads. "Thanks, but we'll walk," I said.

"I do!" Pyper said and climbed in beside her.

The rest of the coven ignored her. They were having way too much fun playing in the snow.

"Merry Christmas," Kane and I said, waving as they took off out of the square.

"Well, *Ms.* Calhoun? Are you ready to go home?" Kane said, nuzzling my neck.

"That's Mrs. Rouquette to you, buddy," I teased, slipping my hand into his. I hadn't officially changed my last name after we got married, but I did love the sound of it.

A slow grin spread over his face. "That's better."

I ran my fingers over his five o'clock shadow. "The faster you get me home, the faster I'll let you unwrap your present."

He raised one eyebrow and scanned my body.

I laughed and nodded. "Yes. There might also be gingerbread cake waiting."

Without a word to the rest of the coven, he tugged me out of the square. Three blocks later we were standing in front of our house with snow kissing the steps and frost tinting the windows.

"It's gorgeous,'" I said.

"Uh huh," he murmured, nibbling my ear.

"You didn't even look at it."

"Don't need to. The only thing I have eyes for is the sexy little witch in the indecent, red-velvet dress."

"It's not indecent," I argued.

"You can't see the thoughts running through my head." And then standing right there on our front porch with the snow still falling all around us, he pulled me to him, snaked one hand under my skirt as he caressed my thigh, and devoured me with a kiss.

When we finally came up for air, I was winded and had no trouble matching his indecent thoughts. Too impatient to find my house key, I reached behind me, grabbed the door knob, and unlocked it with a simple zap of magic. "I already got my Christmas present. It was lovely, by the way. Now it's time for me to give you yours."

His eyes glittered as he leaned in and touched his lips to mine. "Best. Christmas. Ever."

A BOURBON STREET VALENTINE

It's Valentine's Day and magic's in the air. Only Kat Hart never expected her handmade jewelry to be at the center of everything. So when her night out at Cupid's Ball turns into a competition to be a handsome stranger's wife, it's up to her to break the spell…or she might get more than she bargained for.

CHAPTER 1

"*I* need something that's going to be a panty-dropper." The sweaty middle-aged man pumped his eyebrows and leered at me. "Know what I mean, red?"

The shop spotlights glared off his balding head, making me squint as I tried to hide my distaste. We were in my studio gallery, Silver Kat Jewelry, and if I hadn't needed to pay rent, I'd have refused to sell him anything. Unfortunately, that wasn't an option. Bourbon Street wasn't cheap. Clearing my throat, I pointed to a pink diamond ring, set into a tasteful rose gold setting. "This style has proven to be a popular seller."

He pressed his lips together into a tight line. "Christ, red. That's a lot of zeros in that price tag. I didn't even spend that much on the wife."

Bile rose up in the back of my throat. The last thing I wanted to do was sell this jackass one of my handmade pieces of jewelry.

"I see. Maybe I should direct you to this case—"

The bell on my shop door chimed and a handsome,

though relatively short man, strode in wearing a purple-velvet coat, black slacks, and stylish fedora hat. "Good morning. How is my favorite jeweler today?"

"Good?" I gaped at the stranger, watching him stroll from case to case nodding his approval. He exuded confidence and had sex appeal to spare.

He picked up a three-tiered chainmail necklace with an amber pendant. "Lovely. Truly remarkable."

A small bubble of warmth grew in my chest. It was always nice to have one's work admired, especially by a handsome stranger. Hey, just because I had a boyfriend, didn't mean I couldn't look, right? I wasn't dead. "Are you looking for a gift for your special someone?"

The customer in front of me cleared his throat, clearly irritated. "I was here first."

The man in purple velvet smiled at him. "Of course you were. But don't worry. I'm not here to purchase anything. I'm making a delivery." He turned his attention to me. "Kat Hart?"

"Yes?"

"Happy Valentine's Day." He held out a small package wrapped in shiny royal blue paper.

Delivery man? He was kidding right? He should be modeling for romance covers. I held my hand out eagerly. There was no doubt the gift was from my boyfriend Lucien. He'd been too busy working during the last week for us to spend much time together, but I should've known he wouldn't forget Valentine's Day.

The man placed the box into my palm, his warm fingers barely brushing my wrist. A small shock zapped me and I jumped back, clutching the present. "Ouch."

"Sorry. Static." He tipped his hat and headed for the door.

After a few steps, he turned back. "Your admirer was insistent that I get it to you this morning. I think he wants to make sure you feel special all day."

The door chimed and he was gone.

My fingers twitched to rip open the package, but I put it under the counter and gave my impatient customer my full attention. "Did you find anything you'd like to see?"

"Aren't you going to open your gift?" He leaned casually against the counter, his rush apparently forgotten.

I waved a hand. "I can do that later. It's no big deal."

"Sure it is. Go on. Open it. Besides, I could use some inspiration for what a woman your age would like." He dropped his gaze to my cleavage, that ridiculous leer back on his face.

A shudder of disgust ran through me, and I pulled the box out just to try to speed up his departure. Tearing gingerly at the gorgeous blue wrapping paper, I spied the robin's-egg-blue gift box peeking through. I grinned and discarded the rest of the paper.

"Big spender," my customer said with a sneer.

I ignored him and slowly pulled the top off. An audible gasp escaped my lips as I stared down at the Edwardian-style antique drop-pendant. Set in white gold, the large ruby center stone, was surrounded by a circle of flawless diamonds. It was gorgeous. And it must've cost a fortune.

I nimbly clasped the gorgeous bauble around my neck. The precious metal was warm against my skin and made me tingle and feel special in a way I hadn't ever felt before. Of course no one had ever given me such a beautiful gift before either.

The balding man in front of me let out a frustrated grunt. "Elle's ass isn't that hot. Diamonds are not on the agenda."

It was tough, but I somehow managed to not roll my eyes at the jackhole in front of me. "Maybe something unique then?" I pulled out a silver cuff that had an E. E. Cummings poem etched on it.

He frowned and started to shake his head, but as soon as I handed it to him, his entire demeanor changed. The tension eased from his shoulders, and a relieved smile lit his face. "Just the right price. Does that include gift wrap?"

I gave him a tight smile. It did usually, but for him I was making an exception. "That's an extra five dollars."

"Never mind. I have a grocery bag that will work just fine."

Of course he did. I hurried and completed his purchase. When the bell chimed, indicating he was gone from the store, I let out a sigh of relief, grabbed my phone, and hit Lucien's name. His phone rang four times before it went to voicemail.

"Lucien," I gushed. "Thank you so much. I just got your gift, and it's gorgeous. You really shouldn't have. But I love it. It's perfect. I'll see you tonight. Have a good day."

I hit 'End' and tucked the phone into my back pocket just as the door chimed again. A clean-cut man wearing a gray suit rushed in, carrying a coffee cup with the words, *The Grind,* scrolled across it. I grinned. He'd been to my friend Pyper's café, just a couple blocks down the street.

"Good morning." I unconsciously moved three steps to the right, stopping in front of my silver bracelet display. My gaze landed on a hammered, sterling silver cuff that had the word passion engraved on the back.

"I need a gift for my girlfriend. We're having breakfast in five minutes and if I show up empty handed, it's going to be ugly." Sweat popped out on his forehead as he fidgeted with his credit card.

I pulled the cuff out of the case. "This is the one."

He picked it up and frowned as he inspected it.

"Turn it over," I said, knowing without a doubt this was the perfect item for him.

His expression turned from skeptical to surprised delight when he read the inscription. Then he looked up and smiled at me. "That was amazing. How did you know?"

I shrugged, having no earthly idea. The piece had just jumped out at me. And he was happy, so I was happy.

Humming to myself, I rang him up and passed him the bag. Just before he left, I added, "Oh, wait. Take one of these." Holding out a flier for a fundraiser to keep the Mystic Theatre in business, I smiled. It was a gorgeous place that had been built in the nineteen twenties. "If you really want to knock her socks off, take her to Cupid's Ball tonight. It's the event of the year, and there will be a gourmet buffet."

"Hmm, that would solve my reservation problem." He grabbed the flier and nodded his appreciation. "Thanks."

The moment he slipped out the door, another customer hurried in. He was tall and gangly, with tattoos covering both arms and gauges in his ears.

"Of course I got you something, Esme baby," he said into his iPhone while scanning my cases. "I got it weeks ago."

A vision of a dark-haired girl, dressed in a black lace tank top, poufy black tulle skirt, and spiked lace-up boots flashed in my mind. She wore zero jewelry, but had long elegant fingers. I imagined the pair of them hanging out back stage with the band at a rock concert.

Reaching beneath the counter, I pulled out my newest creation; a large midnight-purple flower ring, covered in sparkling Swarovski crystals. I'd just finished it the night before and hadn't yet put it out. I whispered, "How about something like this?"

He studied it, then a slow smile lit his angular face as he spoke into the phone. "Babe, you're going to love it. Relax." Without missing a beat or even asking the price, he whipped out his credit card and mouthed, *Gift wrap, please.*

A few minutes later when he was off the phone, he grabbed the wrapped box, stuffed the receipt in his pocket and said, "I don't know how you did that, but you're right. She's going to love it."

I handed him one of the fliers, determined to give one to every customer. If the Art's Council didn't raise enough cash, the Mystic would be sold at auction, and there'd likely be no more theatre with the beautiful frescos on the ceiling. To me, it was the most gorgeous building in the city. "I hope so. Happy Valentine's Day to both of you."

"You, too."

The same thing happened the rest of the morning. Customers came in, and for some strange reason, I felt compelled to recommend different pieces I was sure would be perfect for their significant others. Every one of them took my advice, and within a few hours, my day was already shaping up to be the most profitable of the year.

The morning flew by in a blur, and it wasn't until my stomach growled that I glanced at the clock. It was past one. Geez, no wonder I was starving. I hadn't had anything but a coffee since the night before. I hurried to the front door, flipped the sign that indicated I'd be right back, and slipped out, locking up behind me.

On my way to the sandwich shop, Lucien called.

"Happy Valentine's Day, gorgeous," he said, a smile in his tone.

"I got my gift. It's just lovely. Thank you." I fingered the pendant as I hurried into a nearby sandwich shop.

"You're welcome. I—dammit. Kat, can I call you back? One of the council witches just walked into the lab."

"Of course. Or I'll just see you at six-thirty." I smiled at the impatient worker behind the deli counter and muttered, "The usual."

He nodded and went to work.

"Six-thirty," Lucien confirmed, and clicked off.

The line went dead, and I wondered what emergency was happening at the Witch's Council. Lucien had recently taken a job in the archives department. But more often than not, he was asked to help out when the caseworkers were overloaded. Since he was the second in command for New Orleans coven, he had a lot of practical skills. I just hoped he wasn't dealing with any black magic.

A shudder ran through me, and I shook my head, trying to force the thought from my mind. He'd be fine. This wasn't his first rodeo.

With my sandwich and soda in hand, I hurried back to my shop and sighed when there was a line five people deep outside the door. The bank account would be happy, but my stomach was going to have to wait.

"Miss Hart?" A man in jeans and a T-shirt said, holding a giant bouquet of roses.

"Yes?"

"Delivery." He pushed the long-stemmed, pink roses into my arms. "Happy Valentine's day."

I stood there like an idiot, staring at the bouquet. The

pendant had been more than enough. Then I tore open the card and grinned. *Only the best for my girl, love Lucien.*

With a bounce in my step, I opened the door, dropped the flowers into a nearby vase, stored my lunch, and went to work helping all the last-minute shoppers make sure they didn't end up in the doghouse when they got home.

CHAPTER 2

*J*ade, my best friend, held the door open for me and swept her arm out in a royal fashion. "After you, milady."

We'd both been stood up. Lucien had sent a text letting me know he was still tied up in Council business and was going to be late—if he even made it at all. Jade's husband, Kane, a demon hunter, was also out on a call. Holidays were always the worst for the paranormal protectors of the city. They seemed to bring the worst out in some people.

I laughed at Jade's poor attempt at an English accent. "Who are you supposed to be? Hugh Grant?"

"No." She shook her head, her long strawberry blond hair flaring out around her. "More like Benedict Cumberbatch."

I shook my head, still chuckling. "Needs work. But he would've been an acceptable substitute."

"Right?" She slipped her arm through mine and we strolled into the Mystic Theatre.

The seats had been removed, leaving a large ballroom lit with a series of crystal chandeliers. Tables were set up around the perimeter of the room, where guests were already enjoying elegantly crafted hors d'oeuvres.

"Over there." Jade pointed at the buffet at the back of the room. "I need food before I pass out. It's been a hectic day."

"Lead on, wise one." My stomach growled just thinking about it. The half-eaten sandwich I'd had for lunch was long gone.

We took our time perusing the multitude of gourmet cheeses, fancy salads, and seafood choices. Not to mention drooling over the chocolate pots de crème and toffee crumble cheesecake. But we stuck with artichoke salads, tuna tartare, and filet medallions. The desserts could wait. Or so I thought.

Halfway from the buffet to our table, Jade and I were suddenly cut off by a half-dozen women, their eyes bright and lips curved into pleased smiles.

"Ms. Hart?" a short blonde in a sparkling silver dress asked.

"Yes?" I glanced around, my gaze landing on a thin brunette with wild, curly dark hair. She wore a lace-covered bustier with a purple leather skirt, and spiked knee-high boots. I did a double take and instantly searched for the large, purple floral ring. It was right there on her left hand.

Whoa. She was Esme, the girl I'd envisioned with the tattooed guy earlier in the day. A chill ran up my spine. At the time, I'd had no idea I'd been having a vision. I'd thought the girl was just someone I'd imagined him with.

"I'm Elle. I wanted to let you know your work's amazing," the blonde gushed, holding out her arm. She wore the etched silver bracelet that I'd sold to the two-timing sleazebag earlier that morning.

"Uh, thanks." Curiosity took over as I realized they were

all wearing pieces I'd sold that day. How in the world did they all know each other? Had an entire office staff done their shopping with me? "Looks like y'all are having a great Valentine's Day."

"Thanks to you," they said in unison, as they collectively took a step forward, closing ranks around us. Each of them lovingly touched the piece of jewelry they'd received that day. Their expressions were...off; too happy, as if forced.

I gave Jade a what-the-hell look and cast my gaze toward our table, indicating we should get the heck out of there. These ladies were doing a weird interpretation of the Stepford Wives.

She grinned at me, clearly not as alarmed as I was. In fact, not alarmed at all, even though a group of women I'd never met had accosted us.

I widened my eyes at Jade, but she was laughing at something the curly-haired blonde wearing the hammered cuff had said.

"Gosh, Kari, I'd have kicked him out of bed, too." Jade covered her mouth to control her laughter.

I tugged on her arm, unease making me back away. "Thanks, everyone. I'm truly honored you're pleased with your pieces, but if you'll excuse us, Jade and I are going to take our seats." I lifted my plate, indicating it was time to eat. "You should really grab some dinner before it gets too picked over."

Together, they all took a step back, and nodding, they immediately headed toward the buffet line. Jade said nothing as I led her toward our designated table.

When we sat down, I stared at her. "What's going on?"

She stabbed a piece of steak with her fork. "What do you mean?"

"Those women. Don't you think something was a little weird?"

She let out a tinkling laugh. "Oh, Kat. No. They were all filled with love. It was radiating off them. It was beautiful actually."

I frowned at her, noting her eyes were too bright and her smile was too wide. I snapped my fingers in front of her face. "Enough. You're freaking me out."

She blinked and shook her head, confusion replacing her Stepford expression. "Weird."

"No kidding. Want to tell me what that was all about?"

"I...whoa. I have no idea." Jade picked at her tuna, but didn't eat.

I stuffed a forkful of the artichoke in my mouth, and after I swallowed, I asked, "Is it a spell of some sort?"

She pursed her lips. "I'd feel it if it was, wouldn't I?" Jade was a powerful white witch and the leader of the New Orleans coven. If anyone could feel a spell in the air, it was her.

"I'd think so."

"All I feel is happiness and affection." She turned her attention to the group of women who'd settled just a few tables away, her eyes going soft and unfocused for just a second. "No. They aren't witches. There isn't any power radiating from them. Maybe it's just that their energy was rubbing off on me."

That was possible. Jade was also an empath, and if she wasn't careful, other people's emotions infiltrated hers. Blocking emotions out was always tougher in crowds and tended to deplete her reserves. I touched her arm, letting her know I was there if she needed an energy boost. I'd shared my energy with her many times over the years when she'd needed it.

This time she placed her hand over mine and shook her head. "Thanks, but really, I'm fine."

"Okay. But I'm here if you need me."

She tightened her fingers around my hand and stared at me. "Weird."

"What?" I popped a crab puff into my mouth.

"Your energy, it's a little heavier. Like—"

"There you are!" Mary Ann Wasserman cried, hurrying toward us. She wore a bright, red-velvet dress and had diamonds dripping from her ears, wrists, and neck. She was the chairwoman of the board that was working to save the theatre. "I need to borrow Kat for a few minutes," she said to Jade.

"Of course." Jade picked up her Champagne glass and drank half the contents.

I stood. "What do you need, Mary Ann?"

"Someone to get the dancing started after I make the announcements. Eros is asking for you." She spun and hurried over to the small makeshift stage near the long rows of silent auction tables.

"Who's Eros?" Jade asked.

I shrugged and followed Mary Ann.

CHAPTER 3

"Now that the silent auctions have been completed, it's time to get this party started!" Mary Ann announced. "But remember, the cash bar is still open, and all funds raised will be donated toward restoring this beautiful landmark. So drink up." She glanced around and then added, "But be safe. Cabs will be waiting when the ball ends."

A loud applause rose from the thickening crowd.

"Now in the iconic words of Kevin Bacon, 'Let's Dance!'"

I shook my head and laughed. I was willing to bet at least half the guests had no idea which movie she was referring to.

And just like that, a shimmering disco ball appeared from the ceiling, and a short man in a familiar purple-velvet jacket was taking my hand.

"Where did you come from?" I asked, staring at the gorgeous delivery man who'd brought me Lucien's gift that morning.

He gave me a mysterious smile and stopped in the middle

of the dance floor, bowing with his hand out. "I'm Eros. May I have this dance, Ms. Hart?"

"Uh…oh. Right." Mary Ann had said Eros asked for me. How had it come to be that this unusual man was both my delivery guy and the master of ceremonies of this event?

The man stared up at me, a gleam in his eyes. "I promise to not step on your toes."

He was so serious, I couldn't help but laugh. I curtsied and inclined my head as if we'd been transported back in time. "It would be my pleasure."

Taking my hand in his, he placed the other on the small of my back, and with the ease of Fred Astaire, he proceeded to twirl me around the room.

"So graceful," he said. "Your husband is a lucky man."

I shook my head and showed him my empty left hand. "Boyfriend. But you're right. He is lucky. Not many girlfriends would be so understanding after getting stood up on Valentine's Day."

He frowned. "Stood up?

I gave a tiny shrug. "He had to work."

"On Valentine's Day?" There was disapproval in his darkening eyes.

"It's not a big deal. It happens."

"It shouldn't. Not on this night. The night for lovers." The music slowed, and Eros pulled me closer, swaying to the soulful tune. "Forget about him. I'll be your date."

A tingle of warmth filled my belly, and for some reason, his words took all my worries away. I was at the ball in the arms of a charming man who knew what he was doing on the dance floor. It didn't even matter that he was at least four inches shorter than me. What more did I need?

"She's too good for him," Eros said, nodding to the blonde —Elle—and her married date.

I raised my eyebrows, surprised. "You know them?"

"I know he's married. And that his wife is at home with a sick kid." The derision in his tone was unmistakable.

"Bastard," I muttered. "He was a real ass when he came into my shop today, as well."

His eyes narrowed as he glared at the man. But then the rocker chick and her tattooed boyfriend glided past us, and Eros turned his attention to them, a pleased smile claiming his face.

"You're such a romantic," I teased, patting his lapel.

He gave me a wry smile. "You have no idea."

"Then you'll love this couple." I nodded toward one of my regular customers. Trish was a lifetime jewelry lover and stopped by my shop no less than once a month. Her boyfriend of the week was holding her tightly as she beamed up at him, the sapphire blue earrings he'd purchased from me only a few hours ago dangling from her lobes. He was wearing a seersucker suit and looked quite the southern gentleman. "They've only known each other a few weeks, but I think he might be the one."

Eros studied them, his eyebrows drawing together in concentration. "Not likely. The signs are already there. I'd give it another week at best."

"Huh? What signs?" It was true Trish hadn't had any lasting relationships since I'd known her, but this one...he was into her. Totally. And she certainly appeared to be into him. Unlike the last two she'd brought into the shop.

He shook his head. "Chemistry's off."

"Well, I think they look wonderful together."

Eros twirled me around, and I realized we were closed in

on all sides by the six women wearing my pieces and their dates. My pendant, the one Lucien had given me, heated up against my skin to the point of almost burning me.

I let out a gasp and reached for it, but Eros grabbed my hands, stopping me.

"It's time," he said.

"Time for what?" I cringed back, trying to separate my bare chest from the burning pendant. What the hell was going on?

"For the festivities to begin." His arms tightened around me just as the music stopped. The lights went out, flickered back on, and then winked out again.

A collective gasp went up around the room as I pulled back, trying and failing to get away from him. "Let go!"

"Relax, Katrina. I won't let anything happen to you."

The smooth caress of his words calmed me, and even though in the back of my mind I knew everything should feel very wrong, it didn't. Eros would keep me safe, no matter what happened. I relaxed into him, content and no longer bothered by the heat of my pendant.

The din of the crowd grew louder the longer the lights were off, and then from across the room, I heard Jade cry, "*Lucerna!*"

The ballroom lit with what looked like thousands of floating candles.

The guests let out a collective gasp of delight, while I stared into the gleaming eyes of Eros. His grip tightened on my wrist, and the half-dozen women wearing my jewelry were now in a tight circle around us, their dates missing.

I saw no one else except Eros and his all-too-willing harem.

"Good," he said, smiling into my eyes. "Are you ready?"

"For?"

His smiled widened as he snapped his fingers, and just like that, everything changed. The crowd, the theatre, Jade, everyone was gone, and the only ones left standing were me, Eros, and the six other women.

"Welcome home, ladies," Eros said, waving a hand around the old New Orleans home. The foyer had Italian marble columns and matching tile. It was as if we'd been transported to a villa in Tuscany. "I look forward to getting to know each of you and eventually choosing my new bride."

CHAPTER 4

A squeal went up around me, and although there was a faint, nagging sense of unease still in the back of my mind, I smiled at him. "Why us?" I asked, genuinely curious.

"Because you, my dears, are the loveliest ladies in New Orleans, the city of my heart." He waved a hand and a gray-haired man dressed in a suit appeared with a tray of Champagne and a small bouquet of red roses.

"Please make yourselves comfortable," Eros said, leading us through the French doors out into the marbled courtyard. A gorgeous infinity edge pool with a waterfall was at one end while a white gazebo covered in lush vines was at the other.

"Oh wow," Trish said with a happy sigh, her sapphire earrings sparkling in the shimmering moonlight.

"There are bathing suits in the pool house." Eros strode over to the end of the pool and sat in a throne-like high-back chair that was covered in blooming jasmine.

It occurred to me the flowers must be spelled because I'd never known jasmine to bloom in February, at least not in

New Orleans. The fact that I realized he was magical in some way should've bothered me, or at least set a warning bell off, but for some reason it didn't. We were in a beautiful house, with a charming host, and all I wanted to do was enjoy it.

"Please get changed, and then we'll start." Eros plucked one of the roses from the tray and twirled it between his fingers.

I followed the other girls into the pool house, happy to oblige our host. It was only eight o'clock after all, and hanging out in one of the fanciest homes in New Orleans was hardly a hardship. There were three racks of bikini bathing suits in numerous styles for us to choose from. They even still had the tags on them.

I pulled a blood-red number and quickly changed, pleased I'd had a wax recently in anticipation of the holiday.

"Don't forget your heels, ladies," a woman in a sleek, black business suit said. Her raven hair was piled high on her head, and she wore slim wire-framed glasses. She had a no-nonsense look to her, as if she was the house manager.

I stuffed my feet into a pair of matching red, five-inch heels with red soles and thought I'd die of pleasure. The Italian shoes made my feet feel as if they'd been swaddled in the finest Egyptian cotton. "Oh, my. I could get used to this."

"I was *born* for this, honey," Esme, the rocker goddess, drawled as if she'd just walked off the plantation. Her suit was copper with flecks of gold and so small, that if she made one wrong move there was going to be a major wardrobe malfunction. But her skin was honey-colored and flawless. If anyone should be flaunting the goods, it was her.

The seven of us, led by the house manager, walked out of the pool house in a line and around the pool to where Eros was sitting, as if we were in the Miss America pageant.

A slow smile spread over his face, and that gleam was in his eye again. He'd changed as well and was wearing deep-plum board shorts and flip flops. And holy geez, who knew he was sporting a six pack under that purple suit.

He stood and moved to the edge of the waterfall, leaning casually against the stone border. "Now that we're all more comfortable, maybe each of you can name one interesting fact about yourself as an ice breaker."

"What a lovely idea," a curvy, raven-haired woman said. "Hi, I'm Mina and I'm a fashion model for Bianca's Divas. The store specializes in forties and fifties fashion. I have a closet to die for. Actually three closets. All at half price." She waggled her eyebrows and cast the rest of us a superior look. "I swear my dress collection is rivaling my shoe habit. My ex liked to buy my affection."

Esme gave her a tight smile, but the rest of us largely ignored her.

"Thank you, Mina," Eros said, frowning a little.

"I'm the lead singer in a rock band," Esme said, flipping her long dark hair over one shoulder. "Last summer we toured with Black Magic Witches. Thirty cities in thirty days. It was intense."

"Do you play guitar?" Eros asked.

She nodded. "Also the drums. I could jam for days."

"That's so cool," I said to her, rubbing my temple. There was a pulse just above my right eye that was making me slightly nauseated. "I'd love to come see your show."

She frowned and appeared troubled. "Weird. I can't remember when the next gig is."

Eros cleared his throat. "Ms. Hart? Can you tell us something about yourself?"

"Sure. I'm Kat. I was born in Idaho, but moved to New

Orleans for college and never left. I'm a jeweler, specializing in silversmithing. Creating is...well, it's my first love." I stared down at the marble tile, the pounding in my head growing stronger. A vision of a handsome male face with vibrant green eyes flashed in my mind, but I couldn't place who he was. My unease grew, and without another word, I sat down in one of the wrought-iron chairs.

The introductions continued, but I barely listened to the chatter. Something was very off.

"Kat?" Eros stood in front of me, his voice soft.

"Yes?"

He dropped his warm hand to my shoulder and lightly caressed my bare skin. With his touch, my headache vanished and a small spark of energy rushed through me, perking me right back up.

I stood, feeling awkward when I realized the other girls were all staring at me, their eyes flashing in... was that anger?

He handed me one of the red roses and without any preamble, said, "Congratulations, you've made it to the next round."

My fingers closed around the stem automatically, but I stood there dumbfounded. "Next round of what?"

But he moved on without answering me.

Esme, holding her own rose, moved to my side and whispered, "We're all in competition for Eros. At midnight, he's going to pick his future wife."

CHAPTER 5

$\mathcal{T}$he first round ended with Mina, the fashion model with the enviable shoe collection, eliminated. The remaining six of us stood there, awkwardly holding our roses, as Eros held out his hand to the dejected woman.

Her bottom lip quivered, and a fat tear rolled down her face. "But, I'm the prettiest one here. Everyone else is... just average. I mean come on. Esme? What kind of name is that anyway? She needs a hair treatment STAT. And the redhead? The jeweler? Look at her nails. Do you really want someone with such ugly cuticles touching you?" A tiny shudder ran through her as she stared at me.

Ouch. She wasn't wrong. A manicure lasted less than twenty-four hours in my line of work, but that was no reason to put me on blast.

"That wasn't very nice," Elle said, her lips forming a small frown that looked more like a pout. "I think everyone here is gorgeous. Including you."

"Oh, stuff it, blondie."

"Hey," I said, holding my "ugly" hands up. "There's no reason to be obnoxious."

"I'm obnoxious?" Mina gave Elle a look reserved for someone who'd been presented with dog crap. "She's the one who dates married men."

"What?" Elle said, shock flashing through her wide eyes. "No I don't. I'd never—"

Mina flung her hands up and pushed Elle.

The petite woman flew backward and teetered dangerously on the edge of the pool, and then, as if in slow motion, she plunged into the water. She came up sputtering, her mascara running down her face and her gorgeous jewel-studded shoes waterlogged.

"Oh, my." I rushed to the edge to give Elle a hand.

"What the hell was that about?" I heard Esme demand behind us.

"I don't tolerate cheaters," Mina said in a superior voice.

"And I don't tolerate bitches."

I turned around just in time to see Esme yank on Mina's hair. The rejected woman gave a cry of rage as her luxurious head of raven hair flew off, revealing matted, mousy-brown locks plastered to her head.

"I knew that hair was fake," Esme said, holding the wig in two fingers as if it were a dead rat. "Just like those boobs and lips."

Mina slowly straightened, grabbed her wig, and started to stalk off into the house. As she did, the left side of her bikini bottom slid into the most unattractive wedgie, revealing a ghostly white buttock. Her almost-orange tan was so dark, the contrast was startling.

"Someone's been abusing the self-tanner," Kari said in my ear.

I did my best to not laugh out loud. She really did look ridiculous.

Mina started wiggling her hips and hobbling, as if she was trying to de-wedge without picking the fabric from her crack. But it only made matters worse as the other side rode up and both butt cheeks jiggled in the slight breeze.

"Talk about a full moon. Though this one has more dimples than—" Esme started.

Her remaining words were drowned out by laughter, as Mina flipped us all the bird right before she vanished into thin air.

"Oh, gods," I gasped out, barely able to breathe. "Is she going to turn up at the ball like that?"

Eros nodded, sending us into hysterics. He turned to the house manager. "Please take Mina her gown and make sure she gets home safely."

The woman nodded, her expression never changing. And with a snap of her fingers, she was gone, too.

"That was... unkind, ladies," Eros said, with an air of disapproval.

I sobered, but wasn't all that concerned about Mina as I wrapped my arm around a shivering Elle. "She deserved it. Poor Elle is freezing."

"She was a fake bitch," Esme said, not pulling any punches. "You should've heard her in the dressing room when we were changing. Very selfish. And what she said and did to Elle was way over the line. I, for one, am not sorry."

The other girls nodded their agreement.

Eros sighed, but didn't disagree. "Let's just move on shall we?"

Elle's teeth started to chatter as the breeze picked up. "Can we get a towel or something?" I asked him.

"Come with me." He grabbed Elle by the hand, but before they left, he gestured to the pool house again. "Get changed and meet us in the game room. I have a surprise for everyone."

CHAPTER 6

The five of us changed quickly into yoga pants and form-fitting T-shirts that had been left for us, and then we shuffled into what Eros called the game room. Only it wasn't a game room at all. It was a commercial kitchen that looked like a set out of a televised competition show, complete with stainless steel work stations and commercial stove-top ovens.

"Welcome back, ladies." Eros had his arm around a rosy-pink Elle. She was also dressed in yoga attire, along with a deep-purple hoodie sweatshirt. It practically swallowed her petite frame, leaving no doubt it belonged to Eros.

"I don't cook," Esme said, placing her hands on her hips.

"Me neither," Trish added, mirroring her stance.

Eros released Elle, much to her dismay. The forlorn look on her face made me want to roll my eyes. He strode over to Esme and Trish, taking them both by the hand. "Not an issue ladies."

They both leaned into him, their heads close to his as if the trio was discussing something in strict confidence. After a moment, Esme let out a happy laugh and Trish grinned, her face flushing bright red.

"Better?" Eros asked them.

They both nodded and happily took their places behind their work stations.

"You're going to love this," Esme said, piling her dark hair into a bun on top of her head.

"Ladies, I have something special to help you out with your baking." He turned toward a large mirror covering one wall, raised his arms high in the air, and waved as if beckoning someone.

We stood there in silence, while Trish fluffed her short black hair and…what was she doing? Gads. She was sucking her stomach in while pulling her v-neck T-shirt down, revealing even more of her already ample bosom. My goodness, she had quite the rack. I glanced down at my own modest chest and wondered if those breast creams that were advertised on late night TV really worked. Maybe a spell. I'd make a note and ask Jade about magical breast augmentation. Just a cup or two sizes bigger would do the trick.

"Kat," Esme whispered. "Why are you scowling at your left tit? Did it insult the right one or something?"

I jerked my head up just in time to see six perfectly-sculpted gods walk right through the mirrored wall wearing nothing but aprons tied around their waists.

"Holy abs," Trish breathed.

"Abs? Look at those perfect pecs." Esme took a step forward with her hand out as if she was going to sample one.

My mouth went dry as a tall, blond, Greek God stepped up next to me, his apron so low I could see the outline of his V cut disappearing into his groin area. I suppressed a groan.

Good goddess. I'd never seen anything hotter. Perfection in an apron. I eyed him up and down, and then before I could stop myself, I said, "Turn around."

The corner of his mouth lifted in an amused, knowing smile, but after scanning my body with a searing gaze, he did as I asked.

Much to my relief and disappointment, he was wearing black boxer briefs. But they still showed off quite the perfect backside.

I licked my lips.

"Focus, ladies," Eros said. "The men will be your baker's assistants. Use them in any way you see fit—"

Multiple snickers cut him off.

He cleared his throat. "Ahh, I meant use their knowledge and skills about baking. Save the rest for after the competition. All right?"

"Yes, sir!" Esme saluted him, while the other girls expressed their agreement.

I stood there, staring at my assistant, that uneasy feeling coming back to me. Something niggled at the back of my mind, and I felt like I'd forgotten something. There was something I was supposed to do or remember, only I couldn't put my finger on it.

"Kat." Eros casually slipped his arm over my shoulders. "This is Bradley. He's an expert in all things chocolate. Make something divine."

The unease slipped away, but the nagging doubts lingered.

"How about warm-center chocolate cakes?" Bradley asked, his voice so rich and smooth, I nearly melted at the sound of it.

"Okay," I breathed.

He chuckled, clearly used to being ogled. "Let's go, Kitty Kat. We have chocolate to melt."

I happily followed him and every instruction he gave me. It was more like he was doing the baking and I was the helper, but that was perfectly fine with me. To be honest, I paid more attention to the muscles rippling beneath his apron than I did anything else—until Esme screamed and jumped back from her stove.

Hot sugar boiled over the saucepan and kept right on going down the front of the stove.

"Turn it off," her helper ordered.

"I can't. It just keeps growing." She had powdered sugar in her hair and a smudge of chocolate on her cheek and was straight-up panicking. "I'm going to burn the house down. " She grabbed a bag of flour and threw it at the stove. White powder went up in a giant dust cloud, completely coating the sugar mess, the pot, and the stove. Not to mention me.

"Hey! Watch it." I patted at my shirt, but it was too late. My black shirt was a goner. The only saving grace was that my dessert was already in the oven, safe from her destruction.

"Sorry." She grimaced and finally reached over to turn off her stove. She turned to her assistant. "Any other ideas?"

He glanced around at her mess, then the clock and frowned. "It's too late to cook anything. We'll have to improvise."

The pair retreated and went to investigate the items in the pantry.

"Wow," Elle said, holding a gorgeous chocolate pecan pie. She nodded toward Esme's station. "That doesn't look promising."

"But that does!" I exclaimed. "Holy chocolate, that smells delicious. What's that spice I smell?"

She smiled. "It's a secret ingredient."

"It's bourbon," Kari said, frowning at her uninspired chocolate chip cookies. "I saw her add it to the pie mixture. And now that I see how nice hers turned out, I think I need a shot."

I turned to Bradley. "How's ours coming?"

He shrugged. "I don't know. Didn't you set the timer?"

"Timer?" Crap. I bit my bottom lip. "Do you know what time we put them in there?"

He shook his head as he walked to our oven. Then he groaned. "I said 375 degrees, not 475."

Oops!

He pulled them out, his face grim. "Not looking good, Kitty Kat."

I peered over his shoulder and let out a groan. The edges were burned. Worse, when he cut into one of the individual cakes, the batter wasn't all the way done.

"Double damn," I said, and dipped my finger into the rich filling. "Maybe no one would notice if we serve them on your abs."

He laughed. "We can always try."

"That's it!" Esme cried, having already returned with a can of whipped cream. "Holden, lie down on the counter."

Her assistant stared at her, one skeptical eyebrow raised.

"Trust me," she said. "We're going to win this challenge."

As the others were placing their desserts on the judging table, Holden climbed up on the counter next to it and held still as Esme went to work. When she was done, Holden had whipped-cream-topped, chocolate-ganache kisses arranged in a heart shape with an arrow through it right on his abdomen.

She waved a hand and bowed as she said, "Voila. My masterpiece is complete."

Eros took one look at her offering and let out a bellow of a laugh. Then he immediately handed her a rose. "You, my dear, are a complete delight."

She beamed and then literally licked one of the kisses off Holden's abs.

I chuckled, while two of the girls scowled.

Elle beamed at her. "Well done, Esme. You're so creative."

"Thanks." Esme slipped her arm through the blonde's and waited with her for the verdict of her dessert. To no one's surprise, it was delicious, and Eros handed her a rose as well.

He moved on to Trish's brownies. They were lovely, sitting there on a fancy plate all cut up into perfect squares. I was certain she'd pass Eros's test, but when he bit into the first one, he gagged and spit the crumbs out, splattering them all over her white shirt. Little specks of chewed up brownie looked like… well, never mind. Let's just say it wasn't pretty.

"What are these?" Eros asked.

Her baker wrinkled his nose and with an air of disgust, he said, "Sugar-free, gluten-free, flavor-free brownies."

"They're healthy!" Trish cried, crossing her arms over her brownie-vomit T-shirt.

"It's Valentine's Day," Eros said. "I think it's a day of indulgence, don't you?"

"One does not keep ninety pounds off by being indulgent!" She tightened her hands into fists and turned bright red.

"Ninety pounds. Wow. That's impressive," I said. "Good for you."

She opened her mouth to speak, but then closed it and gave me a single nod of acknowledgment.

"Impressive indeed," Eros agreed. He inspected the brownies once more, sniffing them. Then he gingerly put a tiny crumb on his tongue. His look told us everything we needed to know. The brownies were garbage bound. "I'm sorry, Trish. I admire your effort and your conviction, but I'm afraid we're not going to be compatible. Healthy desserts are never going to fit in my world view. I'm sorry."

Trish shrugged. "Fine. Where's my gown. I want to get out of these disgusting clothes."

"Ms. Bex will take you." He gestured to the house manager who'd reappeared after making sure Mina got home safely, and the pair of them left the game room.

The other two women didn't fare any better, though their desserts appeared to be at least edible. Eros claimed he was looking for someone a little more adventurous.

When he got to me, I was certain I was going to be sent home. And while my heart seemed perfectly fine with that scenario, there was a strange part of me that was disappointed, a detached part that seemed to have a mind of its own.

So when he handed me a rose without even looking at my dessert, I stared at him in surprise. "I thought for sure I was a goner after this mess."

He winked. "Not everything is as it seems."

CHAPTER 7

The three of us, along with Eros, entered a large, elegant room that appeared to be a formal sitting room. Only the settee, two ornate armchairs, and a coffee table barely managed to fill half the room. The other half was taken up with three large, cloth-covered pedestals filled with candles and other curious items I'd only ever seen at a new age, witch supply store. Potions, feathers, herbs, pestles and mortars were among the curiosities on display.

And of course, there was a single red rose in the middle of each pedestal.

"What's going on?" I asked him, foreboding crashing into me.

"Just one more challenge before I choose my bride," Eros said, patting my arm.

That same warmth and soothing energy flowed through me, but again, the nagging doubts didn't go away.

Magic.

This entire night had been influenced by it. There was no doubt about that. But who was casting the spells? I peered at

Eros. He didn't seem to notice my scrutiny as he brushed a lock of Elle's hair behind her ear. He likely thought I was concerned he was going to choose her.

I wasn't.

I didn't want to be anyone's wife... or did I? A flicker of those green eyes came back to me. So familiar. So comforting. I fought to hold onto the image of those eyes, but a glass was shoved into my hands by Eros.

"Drink, Kat. The liquid will help you relax."

I did as he said without a fight and let the harsh bourbon burn my throat. It felt good to finally feel something real, something that wasn't mild contentment. I downed the rest of the glass, hoping the liquid heat would snap me out of my pliable zombie state.

"Whoa. Slow down." Eros took the glass from me with a kind smile. "You don't want to be drunk for this last test."

I had a feeling I did, but I tried not to scowl. The last thing I wanted was another shot of his brand of comfort.

"This test is to see if any of you have latent magical abilities. I want to see if when you concentrate, you can light a candle with your mind, levitate a rose petal, or mix a potion. Having magic isn't a requirement, but it would help me in my line of work if my partner had some talent in the field."

Esme frowned. "I'm not a damned witch. I'm a musician."

"You could be. One never knows until they try." He slipped his hand into Elle's and escorted her to the middle pedestal.

Esme and I followed, taking our spots beside her.

"Now, the bourbon I gave you? It was laced with a hint of an anti-inhibition potion. If you have any magical talent, it should be easier to tap now. Just concentrate on one candle in front of you and imagine it lit."

The other two women concentrated on their candles, but I couldn't. The pendant on my chest was burning again. The last time was right before we'd been transported from the ball. Was he taking us somewhere else? Not again. I didn't think I could handle it. I cast him a glance, but the vision of the green eyes flashed in my mind again, and this time they came with a face.

Lucien.

The name filtered through my mind, and I swear I heard an answering call. "Kat?"

I twisted, searching for the voice I knew, but sucked in a gasp as the heat from the pendant intensified. "Ouch!" I fumbled with the clasp, trying desperately to remove the necklace. Dammit! Why couldn't I get my fingers to cooperate?

Kat! I heard the desperate cry again, only this time I knew it was in my mind.

Lucien, I answered back. *I'm here.*

Break the spell. I know you can do it.

Beside me I heard the delighted gasp of Elle and noticed the flicker of candlelight.

"Excellent!" Eros said, pleasure turning his voice to velvet.

I turned just in time to see him holding out a blood-red rose to her. She reached out and her fingers were almost around the stem when I wrapped my hand around the pendant and yanked, breaking the chain. The fiery stone seared a burn into my hand, but I didn't care. The spell, it was the pendant. Eros had given it to me. I'd seen Esme in a vision after I'd put it on and known exactly what jewelry piece each woman would want.

167

Everything was tied to the pendant. Hadn't Jade said my energy was a little heavy? But I'd disappeared off to dance with Eros before she could finish that thought, and I hadn't seen her since.

A flash of light nearly blinded me, startling everyone. And when my vision cleared, I saw Jade and Lucien standing not ten feet in front of me. I nearly cried in relief.

"Destroy it!" Jade ordered as she ducked a blow from Esme.

"How dare you interrupt our Valentine's Day," the rocker bellowed, as she went after Jade with a candlestick.

"Esme!" I shouted, but she didn't listen.

Elle jumped in front of Eros, stopping Lucien from restraining him. "No! You can't. He's the love of my life."

"Step aside, miss. I'm not interested in hurting you," Lucien said calmly, while magic crackled in his palms.

"Kat! The pendant," Jade urged.

I glanced down at the now-cool pendant, then dropped it onto my pedestal and smashed it with one of the heavy stone candlesticks. Sparks shot from the contact point, making me jump back.

Everything stopped.

The surroundings changed from the luxurious Italian villa, to a rundown old Victorian with rotted boards and cobwebs.

"Eww," Esme said, backing up from a round man with cherry red cheeks and golden curls who was standing exactly where Eros had been a moment before. He wore a white toga and golden sandals.

"Cupid," Lucien said to the man, admonishment in his tone.

"Cupid?" Jade and I asked at the same time.

"The name is Eros," he spit out, as he glared at Lucien. "How many times do I have to tell you that?"

Eros? Cupid was the gorgeous man who'd been putting us to the test all night. I shuddered. Holy V-day horrors.

Lucien glared at him then turned to me and put his arm around my waist, pulling me close.

I leaned against his strong, hard body and let out a sigh. "Where were you?"

"Tracking a witch who was selling illegal love potions." He jerked his head toward Cupid. "Turns out Cupid here bought one this morning. I didn't know until about an hour ago when Jade and I finally connected. She's been going out of her mind ever since you disappeared from the ball."

"An hour? What took you so long?" All I wanted to do was go home, take a scalding shower, and forget I'd been spelled to want Cupid. Gah!

"We needed an opening. I finally figured out you were the one that had been spelled, but it took me long enough. The spell was extremely subtle."

Jade used a corner of the table cloth to pick up the pendant, which was still in one piece. Only the spell had been broken. Then she tucked it into her handbag. "For the Witch's Council. They're going to want that."

"Can we go now? Or do you have to do something about him?" I asked, more than ready to be home.

Lucien let out a huff of frustration. "Unfortunately there isn't a law about unknowingly buying an illegal love potion. Since the rogue witch was selling them through a reputable outlet, we're going to have to let him go."

"But if you so much as look at another woman in this city in the wrong way, you're going to have to answer to me," Jade said to Eros, her eyes flashing with power.

"Hey," Elle said in her sweet tone, and took Cupid's hand in hers. As soon as she touched him, he morphed back into the handsome man wearing the purple velvet jacket. Because she was so petite, he was barely an inch taller than her. "Eros was nothing but a perfect gentleman. There's no need to threaten him."

"Other than spelling all of us into competing to be his wife?" I blurted.

"What?" Jade gasped out. "You're kidding me?"

I shook my head. "Bathing suit competition, baking contest, and then the magic test."

Jade's eyes widened. "Swimsuit? Baking? You're kidding me. What was he doing? Looking for a trophy wife?"

"No." Eros put his arm around Elle in a protective manner. "I just wanted to see how they all handled themselves in certain situations. I spend a lot of time around desperate people looking for love. Because of that, I have more than my share of women who hit on me. Jealousy was a red flag for me. The swimsuit competition was about seeing how everyone reacted when presented with superficial beauty. I didn't want to be stuck with someone who was insecure. That's why I sent Mina home."

I pursed my lips. "All right. But what about the baking?"

"That was a little selfish on my part. I like sweets." He grinned. "It's why chocolates are a mainstay of Valentine's Day. I do want a woman who knows her way around the kitchen. But I also wanted to see how she dealt with distraction, working with other people, and how she handled herself under a bit of stress." He tightened his hold on Elle. "Not to mention, it just helped me have time to observe some patterns."

"And the magic?" Esme demanded. "What did you want us to do? Spell your man bits to make them bigger?"

Jade chuckled.

I shook my head. "Esme."

"What? He ruined my night with my man. Did you know I'm going back out on the road tomorrow for a week? Zane and I had big plans for that new bed of his. I can't even believe I'm still here. If I had my phone, I'd have called an Uber already." Her face was so red I expected steam to rise from the top of her head.

"My apologies," Eros said, bowing his head to her. "I would send you back immediately, but these two witches have temporarily neutralized my magic."

Elle's eyes widened. "Then how did you morph back into this form?"

"You did it, love," he said, gazing at her like a lovesick puppy. "I only needed the touch of a beautiful witch. That's you."

Jade shot me a questioning look.

I gave her a half shrug. "Elle just found out she has the magic. I think it's a mild case, though."

"Enough!" Esme threw her hands up. "Can we get out of here?"

"We'll be going in a second," Jade told her and turned to Eros. "I want to know why you want your partner to be magical."

He gave her an ironic shake of his head. "That's just it. I want a partner. Someone I can share my work with. Someone who can understand me. Most people I've met don't get it, and after a while, they resent the work I do."

"Well, if you didn't trick people, it might be different," Jade muttered.

I tended to agree with her. "Don't you play matchmaker for a living?"

He shrugged. "Pretty much. It's still a hard job finding the right fit for people and figuring out the perfect time they should meet. It's not like the stories. I don't just shoot someone in the ass with an arrow and instantly fix their love life, you know."

I shook my head. I didn't know. "Is this how you do it? Spell them and let the dude pick from a pack of women?"

"No." He jerked back as if I'd slapped him. "I play matchmaker with a bit of magic. I use my talent to get them to let their guards down. To give someone a chance who otherwise wouldn't be noticed. That's all. And that's pretty much what I did here tonight. Though I admit it was a bit...unorthodox."

"Deceitful is the word I'd use," I said.

"I was thinking something more along the lines of jackass." Esme flipped him off. "You owe me, dude. Big." She turned to Jade. "Ready?"

Jade nodded, pulled her phone out of her pocket, and sent a text. A second later, her phone buzzed and she said, "The coven is ready to bring us back. Esme, Elle, hold hands with Kat. Lucien and I will do the rest."

"I'm not going anywhere," Elle said. She hadn't let go of Eros once during the entire conversation, and now the two were practically glued at the hip.

Jade stared at her, dumbfounded. "But he tricked you."

"He's been a complete gentleman. Better than the jerk I was dating who had a wife! I didn't even know until tonight." A single tear slid down her cheek. "I'd never in a million years knowingly date a married man. I was the last to know, apparently. I've had shitty luck with men, and I know a good one when I see one. So I'm staying. I'll only leave if he asks me to go."

Eros brushed the tear away and gave her a soft kiss on her temple. "You don't have to go anywhere." Then he produced a blue box—the exact same shade as the one I'd opened earlier that day—got down on one knee, held the ring out to her and said, "Will you be my wife?"

"Yes!" she cried and threw her arms around him. "I will be the best wife you've ever seen."

He laughed and scooped her up. "I believe you will."

"I can't even…" Esme started, but despite the derision in her tone, she was smiling at them.

Jade shook her head. "Let's go and leave the lovebirds alone."

EPILOGUE

A Week Later

"*I* told you I'd be on time," Lucien said, casting an appreciative gaze down my body.

I was wearing skin-tight jeans that left very little to the imagination, a halter top blouse, no bra, and spiked boots with four-inch heels. My outfit wasn't exactly rocker-chic, but at least I'd managed to make my man's eyes glitter.

"Only a week late." I winked at him and handed him a ticket. Esme had sent tickets to my shop for her show at the House of Blues, and Lucien and I were using the opportunity to celebrate our own personal Valentine's Day. No one ever said love was reserved only for February fourteenth.

Not even Cupid.

Eros and Elle were already sitting in the front row when we got there, both of them beaming.

"You just have to come to the ceremony," Elle gushed. "It's going to be next February *after* Valentine's Day. You know how busy Eros is that day. And we set a long lead time so we can be absolutely sure this is the right move for both of us. Not to mention I have to order the dress, the cake, flowers, pictures, and…"

I tuned out, letting her ramble about the perfect wedding, and leaned my head against Lucien's shoulder.

"What about you?" he asked.

"What about me?" I tilted my head and smiled up at him.

"Marriage. A wedding. What do you think?"

"I—"

The lights cut out and a spotlight went up on the stage just as Esme bounced out wearing a sheer top over her black lace bra, cut up stockings, a tight leather skirt, and her thigh-high boots. "Good evening everyone. Before we get started, a gentleman in the front row has a question to ask."

I let out a shocked gasp as Esme reached her hand out to me.

"Come on Kat, get your ass up here," she demanded.

A roar of approval went up through the crowd as Lucien followed me to the stage.

I stood there in complete shock as he got down on one knee, holding my hand. Tears filled my eyes before he even got one word out.

"Kat, my love. I think this might have been a long time coming, but on Valentine's Day I saw a man so determined to find his partner, he went to unimaginable lengths to do it. That night I realized with a full heart, I'd already found mine."

"Awww," the crowd said on a sigh.

"And now I want the world to know it, too. Will you do me the honor of marrying me, of being my wife, my partner, my best friend?"

I gaped at him, too stunned to say anything as the tears ran unchecked down my face.

After a few beats, Esme chuckled into her microphone. "Kat, I think this is where you give the man an answer before he has a heart attack."

I glanced at her. She gestured to Lucien who was still kneeling, still staring up at me with a mix of hope and terror on his face.

"Yes!" I blurted.

He jumped up and enveloped me in a crushing hug. "Thank the gods. If you'd said no—"

"I wouldn't have," I whispered in his ear. "I'm yours, completely and totally, forever."

Esme's band started playing *Cupid,* by Amy Winehouse.

Lucien and I both froze, then threw our heads back and laughed.

When we finally caught our breath, Lucien pushed a red curl behind my ear and mouthed, "I love you."

I nodded. "I know. I love you, too."

He let out a breath, brushed my lips with a kiss, and whispered, "Mine."

SPIRITS, HURRICANES, AND THE KREWE OF GHOUL

It's Halloween and Pyper Rayne's all vamped up, ready to play the vampire bride. And so is Ida May, her resident ghost. But when the "vampires" they're partying with start to appear to be real, there's more at stake than just a little bite.

CHAPTER 1

*S*piked boots, a leather corset, and a wooden stake. What else did a girl need for a night out on Halloween? Oh, right. Two puncture wounds on the neck... and maybe a trickle of blood. Yes, that would do it.

"Pyper?" Nissa called, poking her blond head into the back room of the café I owned and managed. "Ready?"

"Just a sec," I said as I pushed my blue-streaked dark hair to the side and expertly added the bite marks and blood to my neck.

"Ida May!" Nissa admonished. "Cut it out."

Chuckling to myself, I shook my head. Ida May was my resident ghost and favorite troublemaker. There was no telling what kind of shenanigans she was up to. I stuffed my lip gloss into the pocket of my skirt and strode out into the front of the café.

"Damn, you look hot," Nissa said.

I studied my new employee. Tiny, but fierce, she was in her early twenties and had large Kewpie doll eyes. When she dressed up, she was a knockout. But the costume she was currently wearing made her look like she belonged in a Fruit of the Loom commercial. "And you look, ah…"

"Ridiculous. It's okay. You can say it. There's no other way to put it when there's a giant strawberry on my head." She adjusted her strawberry-shaped hat that had a straw sticking out of the top of it and then glanced down at her daiquiri-shaped dress. "I can't believe Vince is making us wear these. Why can't I be on the All Vamped Up float with you?"

Every Halloween, the Krewe of Ghoul put on a parade through the French Quarter, and this year, I'd been invited by a client to ride on his vampire-themed float. Nissa was riding in the float sponsored by her boss. Her other boss, that is. She worked part time for the Dollar Daiquiri on Bourbon Street. "Because you're getting paid to ride the Daiquiri Dolls float instead?"

"Right." She frowned. "It still sucks."

I grabbed the tickets I'd stashed in the register and held them up. "I have an extra ticket to the Night of the Living Dead Ball afterward. Wanna come?"

"Really? Omigod, I'd love—" Her dress flew up, exposing her strawberry-print panties. "Hey!"

Ida May cackled behind Nissa. *What the hell is she wearing? Doesn't she know the fellas prefer something a little… I don't know? Sexier? Strawberry Shortcake underwear is just wrong.*

"How do you know anything about Strawberry Shortcake?" I asked Ida May.

Please. I've been watching television since that thing was invented. What else is there to do all day?

"Excuse me?" Nissa glanced around the shop. "Did she just call me Strawberry Shortcake?"

I snorted out a laugh, both relieved and disappointed that

I was the only one who could hear Ida May speaking. She was a ghost from the early nineteen hundreds, and she had been one of the ladies of Storyville—the notorious New Orleans red-light district. To say she had no filter was an understatement.

"Pyper!" Nissa cast a glare in my direction. "It's not funny. Now there's a group of dirty pervs outside staring at me."

"Sorry." I winced, eyeballing a guy making rude gestures with his fingers and tongue.

Please. Nissa should be so lucky to get some much-needed tongue—

"Ida May, you're out of control. If you ever do that to one of my customers, I'm going to get a sage stick, do a cleansing, and toss you out on your ass. Then where will you be?"

No you won't. Life around here would be way too dull without me. She lifted her lacy nightgown and flashed her ruffled panties at me before disappearing into the back room.

She was right. Ida May certainly made the work day a lot more interesting. But I'd never tell her that. The last thing she needed was more encouragement.

"Can we go out the back?" Nissa asked. "I'm afraid I'm going to punch one of those guys if they get within striking distance."

If provoked enough, she'd do it, too. I'd seen her beat the crap out of a cop who'd turned out to be an evil piece of shit. I gave her a sympathetic smile and locked my arm through hers. "Sure thing, Nis. Let's go get our drink on and see where this night takes us."

"Yes, lets." Then she raised an eyebrow and smirked. "Just as long as it's not a daiquiri."

CHAPTER 2

*N*issa and I stood on the corner of Chartres and Elysian Fields in the Marigny neighborhood as the trucks and tractors towing the floats started to line up. The sun was moments from setting, and at sundown, we were scheduled to roll.

"Holy Christ. It's gorgeous," Nissa said as we stared at the All Vamped Up float. It was huge, nearly double the size of the others, with a giant five-tiered wedding cake in the middle. Blood-red roses were strewn across the top and scattered haphazardly over the rest of the tiers, and around the base, black-and-silver rose bouquets decorated the float itself. Everything else was pure white... except for the strategically placed blood stains.

"It's a takeoff on the Bachelor," I explained. "The humans compete for the vampire's affection, and at the very end, the vampire chooses his bride. She's turned at the ceremony, and the undead couple then reign over their human subjects."

"Oh, fun! And all I get to do is throw out these cheesy

things." Nissa held up a button that had a naked pinup girl holding a Dollar Daiquiri.

"Just think of the ball afterward." I pointed to the Walking Dead float behind us. "Looks like there are plenty of hot zombies to choose from."

She eyed the half-dressed group of guys already getting sloshed on cheap beer, and grinned. "Yeah, that tattooed one looks like he's just up my alley."

I gave her a slight nudge. "Go get his number before he's too drunk to remember it."

"Good plan." Waving, she took off down the road, exaggerating the swing of her hips for maximum impact.

"Well, hello there, gorgeous," a man with a husky voice said from behind me.

I turned and spotted Carver Saint, the owner of Fanged, the hottest new jazz club on Frenchmen Street. He had jet-black hair and eyes to match. Normally, he had a quiet, important air about him. But tonight, the man I'd only ever seen dressed in impeccably tailored business suits was wearing black skin-tight leather pants, a black see-through mesh top, and black boots with silver accents. If it weren't for his ghostly colored skin and blood-red lips, he'd look more eighties rocker than vampire. "That's quite the costume you have there."

"Yours is better." He cast a slow gaze down my body, lingering on my exposed thighs before shifting to my neck, and licked his lips, one hundred percent in smoldering-vamp character.

I'd expected nothing less from Carver Saint. He didn't do anything half-assed. "Watch it, Carver. These goods aren't exactly on the market."

"Still with the witch, then?"

I nodded. My significant other, Julius, was on duty with the witch council, and while he knew I was a horrible flirt, he'd undoubtedly be more than a little irritated by the way Carver was practically devouring me with his eyes. "Still happily with the witch."

"I see. My loss." He smiled a campy sinister smile, showing his fake fangs. "But if you end up my vampire bride, I guess he'll have to get over it."

"Well, obviously."

That made him laugh as he held his hand out to me. "Ready to entertain the masses?"

"Always." I slipped my hand into his chilled one and let him lead me onto the elaborate float. Had he just removed his hand from a bucket of ice? 'Cause, damn. It was about as pleasant as a dead fish. Squicked out, I tugged my fingers from his and tucked them into my pocket.

Other women dressed up as potential brides had already started to fill in around the edges of the float. Carver nodded to each one as we passed them and then delivered me to the very front, where there was a small makeshift dance floor.

"Wait here," he said. "I'll be back once we start moving."

A redhead in a strapless dress scowled at me and said in a hushed whisper, "That's the bitch to beat."

I raised both eyebrows in surprise.

Her Morticia Addams-lookalike friend cast me a dismissive glance. "She doesn't look that special. Just another over-the-hill barfly. I wonder what he sees in her."

I took a step toward them, a snarky reply poised on my lips, when a tall college-aged girl with sleek chestnut hair stepped in front of me and gave me a sympathetic smile. "Don't pay them any attention. Both of them think Carver's going to be their ticket to the cush life."

That sucked for Carver, but he'd see right through them, no doubt. "What does that have to do with me? I'm just here for some fun."

She threw her head back and laughed. "Honey, you're the only one Carver's paid any attention to yet, and you're gorgeous—that's why. Not to mention anyone who takes one look at Carver knows he wants you. Bad."

I shook my head. "He's just a client of mine. Besides, I'm already spoken for."

"We'll see." She tossed her hair over her shoulder and glided away, almost as if she were floating. I blinked. But she disappeared behind another cluster of vampire-bride hopefuls who were staring at me open-mouthed.

I ignored them. Why in the world were they all losing their minds? Did they think the bachelor contest was for real? Had Carver offered himself up as a date or something and hadn't told me? Cripes. I didn't want a date. All I wanted to do was ride in the parade, throw some beads and candy, and have some fun.

I'd just have to make sure I wasn't picked. No problem.

A shot was fired off in the distance, followed by a loud cheer from everyone around me. Then the float started to move toward the parade route. I grabbed the front railing to keep from falling on my ass and peered out into the darkness. Twilight had disappeared, and it was time to party.

The willowy chestnut-haired woman was back; only in the moonlight, her skin now appeared chalk-white, and her hazel eyes glowed with hints of electric green and yellow.

"Whoa," I said. "That's some affect. Did you use professional makeup?" I reached out to touch her, but she stepped back out of my reach, shaking her head. Oops. What was I doing? "Sorry, occupational hazard. I'm a body painter. Makeup and special effects are sort of my thing."

"Beware of the one with claws."

"Excuse me?" I said, but she floated away again, seeming to disappear into the ether. "What the..." I shook my head and blinked to find her standing exactly where I thought she'd disappeared. Weird.

"Ah, at last," Carver said as he came up behind me. "The night I've been waiting for all year."

I turned to him, amused. "Halloween is your favorite holiday?"

"Absolutely." His grin was back, but then he sobered as a young man dressed in ripped jeans and a Nirvana T-shirt handed him a cordless microphone. Carver looked him over and frowned. "Why aren't you in costume?"

"I am. I'm a grunge-band groupie. See?" He pointed to his shirt.

"You were supposed to dress up in a vampire costume."

"Why? You didn't."

"Yes, I did." Carver glanced down at his leather pants. "What do you think this is all about?"

"Whatever you say, Billy Idol."

Carver shook his head, clearly exasperated, while I suppressed a laugh. "Pyper, this is my, ah... nephew, Vale. He's the moderator of the event."

I laughed at his hesitation. "Are you sure?" Turning to Vale, I smiled and held out my hand in greeting. "Nice to meet you."

He nodded his acknowledgement and stuffed his hands into his pockets, leaving me hanging. Charming. Then he jerked his head toward the back of the float. "The rest of the party just showed up."

I followed Vale's gaze and spotted at least half a dozen new women, each dressed in vintage clothing from varying time periods. "Whoa, when did they get here?" I asked, utterly enchanted by an elegant woman wearing an ornately embroidered black-and-silver ball gown. Her corset was synched tight to show off her incredibly tiny waist, and her soft flowing curls were piled up on her head, secured with what appeared to be diamond-encrusted haircombs.

"Excellent. Marcella has arrived. Now we can start." Carver turned to face the crowd as he held the microphone near his mouth. "Good evening, my lovelies."

A few of the women cried out Carver's name, more let out wolf-whistles, but most just returned his greeting with a demure, "Good evening."

"In just a moment, the festivities will begin. There will be dancing, sparring, and general vampire mayhem. Our job is to entertain the crowd. The more outrageous the better. Got it?"

"Hell, yeah!" the bitchy redhead said while pumping her fist in the air.

Carver smiled at her. "I like your enthusiasm."

She rewarded him with a wide grin and leaned forward while squishing her boobs together with her upper arms, giving everyone an impressive view of her massive cleavage. But when her halter-style dress gaped open, she was suddenly on full display, nipples and all.

He frowned and gave her a tiny shake of his head, appearing completely unimpressed with her cheap tactics. "Let's save the outrageous behavior for the crowds, shall we?"

I chuckled and was once again treated to a death glare by the redhead and her friend, Morticia. Shrugging, I turned to Carver. "Your subjects seem to be taking this pretty seriously. If you're not careful, you might find yourself in a sticky situation by the end of the night."

"That's why you're here," he said under his breath and winked.

Carver held his hands up, quieting the group. "Near the end of the run, we'll stop the float, and the one young lady who has consistently enchanted the crowd the most will be chosen as my vampire bride. We'll perform the ritual for the crowds, and then my bride will have the pleasure of accompanying me to the Day of the Dead Ball."

That explained everything. They were all competing for a chance at a date with Carver Saint. Well, they were welcome to him. I was meeting Julius at the Ball.

Carver pressed a button on his phone. A second later, a flash of light shone up from the floor of the float, and inside, a hologram of Carver materialized. His mouth was bloody as if he'd just fed, and the unidentifiable bride standing with him had blood staining the front of her white gown. Neither appeared to be bothered by the gruesome mess as Carver pushed a diamond-and-ruby ring onto her finger.

Cheers and high-pitched whistles erupted from the crowd as the women started closing in on us.

Carver glanced over at me. "You first, my dear."

"First for what?" I asked as the float jerked forward.

"This." He whisked me into his strong arms just as a slow jazz number started. "Let's give them a show, Pyper."

"You want to dance for them?" I asked as he pulled me in closer.

He nodded. "Any bride of mine needs to know what to do on the dance floor. You up for it?"

"You bet your vamp ass I am." Dancing, I could do. I'd been on the dance team all through high school and college, and then there was the exotic dancing I'd done to pay the bills. It might not have been respectable, but after dancing practically every day of your life, one learned a few things.

Carver grinned as he began to move. The music filled the night, drowning out all the other chatter around us, and then instinct took over. My feet moved in time with his as he glided me back and forth then spun me out and back in.

"Ready for a lift?" he asked breathlessly between twirls.

I nodded, instantly accepting his challenge. A sparkle of pleasure hit his dark gaze just as he grabbed me by the waist, tossed me in the air, and caught me as I slowly slid down his chest in a seductive dance move.

The music paused for a beat, and our eyes locked. But instead of the easy-going guy I was used to seeing, I saw raw hunger and desire shining back at me. I stiffened and tried to take a step back. But he tightened his grip, keeping me in place.

"Carver, I don't—"

"The dance isn't finished yet, Pyper." The music resumed, only this time, the beat was a half-step faster. Carver spun me out again and broke into a complicated footwork number while still holding on to my hand.

He was a fabulous dancer, and although the look he'd given me had made me uncomfortable, it didn't matter. Not at the moment. Nothing was going to keep my feet still. It was as if I were under a spell and couldn't control myself. My years of training had taken over, and there wasn't anything else to do but dance.

CHAPTER 3

"*M*y goodness, you're a lovely dancer," Marcella drawled. The gorgeous woman in the velvet embroidered dress had made her way over to me as soon as the dance with Carver had ended.

"Thank you," I said, sucking in a breath. "It's been a while since I had such a worthy partner."

Marcella let out a dainty laugh. "Worthy? You flatter our host too much. He only learned to dance because he wanted an excuse to touch the ladies."

"He needs an excuse?" I asked, glancing around at the women all lined up for their "date" with the club owner.

She grabbed a fistful of pumpkin beads and tossed them into the screaming crowds of parade watchers. "Goodness no. Not now, but back in our younger days, people were quite a bit more conservative."

Younger days? She didn't look a day over thirty. We couldn't have been more than a few years apart. "You've known him a long time then?"

"Oh, sure. Years." She handed me a bag of stuffed vampires. "Throw these out. They'll love them."

We stood at the edge of the float for the next ten minutes, taunting the crowd with the dolls, and threw them out to the ones who were the most responsive. I did, however, ignore the pudgy man who kept flashing me his pasty-white chest.

Marcella snickered when I pointed him out, and then she chucked a strand of beads at him, pegging him right in the forehead. He stumbled, nearly taking out two drunken frat guys. The two girls beside the frat guys grabbed for the beads at the same time, creating a vicious tug-of-war, complete with swearing and threats, until the strand broke in half and everyone lost interest.

I shook my head, amazed. "Parade goers are crazy."

"Entertaining, though." The float slowed to a stop as the parade line started to back up, and Marcella pointed at a gorgeous man wearing only a kilt and a sword. He raised his hands in acknowledgement, indicating he wanted her to throw him some beads. Instead, she pulled a silver sharpie out of her pocket, grabbed one of the vampires, and wrote a phone number on its cape.

I watched in silent amazement as she crooked her finger at him, inviting him to move closer to us. He sauntered up to the edge, his movements a little jerky and awkward.

"Climb up," she ordered.

And to my surprise, the Scotsman leaped up on the side and pulled himself over the edge.

"Nice balls!" someone shouted, followed by, "I guess it's true what they say about kilts!"

Holy Christ. He'd just shown the entire crowd his crown jewels.

"Lovely," Marcella said, casting her gaze to take in his well-defined chest. "I bet you're a tasty one."

"There's only one way to find out," he said, taking a step closer.

Her lips twitched into a self-satisfied grin. "If you insist."

Then she closed the distance, and with one hand on his chest and the other inching up his kilt, she leaned in and kissed him.

I swear I saw actual steam rise from the pair of them. Marcella had started it, but the Scotsman was clearly going to finish it. He backed her against the railing and kissed his way down into her ample cleavage.

Heat smoldered in all the right places as I watched them, and I had to look away just to get a grip on myself. "Holy hotness," I whispered.

The wannabe brides around us were whispering in shocked tones, all of them offended on Carver's behalf. "She's here for the contest, and look at her. My God, what a whore."

I whirled around, ready to give whoever was calling my new friend a whore a piece of my mind, but there were too many faces for me to pinpoint where the voice had come from. So instead, I addressed the group. "For Christ's sake. Why is it okay for a bunch of women to compete for one man's affection, but it isn't okay for this one to decide to choose someone else? Marcella is not a whore just because she isn't saving herself for Carver Saint."

Marcella glanced at me, amusement dancing in her eyes. "Thank you, Pyper. Well said." She turned back to her conquest, leaned in, and trailed kisses up his neck. When she got just below his ear, she paused and did something that made the man's eyes roll into the back of his head with obvious pleasure. A second later, he let out a low moan.

She pulled away slightly, whispered into his ear, and then let him go. He bowed to her as if she were royalty, and said, "Thank you, milady."

She nodded, handed him the vampire doll with her number on it, and then waved her hand, dismissing him.

Without another word, he turned and jumped off the float into the crowd of nearly hysterical observers. The men and women alike swallowed him up as they clambered to get closer to Marcella. She'd whipped them into a frenzy with that move.

The float jerked to life again, and Carver appeared out of nowhere beside her. "I see you've been making friends."

She smirked. "Don't I always?"

Some sort of silent communication passed between them, and I started to feel very much like an outsider. Were they a couple? Ex-lovers? Because it was obvious she wasn't competing for the coveted spot of vampire bride.

I was contemplating the best way to make myself scarce when Carver held out his hand to her and said, "I need your assistance with something."

"I very much doubt that," she replied, but took his hand nonetheless.

"Oh, but I do. We're going to spar. And I know how much you love that."

"You're giving me the chance to kick your ass in public?" Her eyes lit with the challenge. "Hell yes."

"I can't wait for this." I laughed, suddenly at ease. They reminded me of my relationship with Kane. They were far too familiar with each other to be casual friends and far too laissez faire about the other's romantic interests to be lovers. No, they were either related or had been friends for years.

"I'm sure you won't be disappointed," Marcella said over

her shoulder, and smiled.

I froze. Where had those fangs come from? She hadn't been wearing them before. And was that... blood staining her mouth?

Her smile fell as she touched her tongue to her pointed fangs. Surprise lit her dark gaze for just a moment before her expression went blank and she clamped her mouth shut, turning her back on me.

"Did you just see that?" I asked the woman standing beside me.

"Yeah. So what? You upset he found someone better to spend his time with?"

I glanced over and spotted Morticia sneering at me with her redheaded friend sending eye darts at my head. Holy Hell. Why hadn't I checked to see who I was engaging with? Just what I needed—Bitter Betty and her grumpy sidekick. "Never mind."

I grabbed the bag of throws Marcella had given me and headed to the other side of the float, praying there was someone sane to stand next to... or at least someone who didn't appear to want to throw me over the edge of the float.

"That's right. Keep walking," Morticia yelled once I was a few feet away.

I'd had just about enough of her BS, and I lifted my hand, sending her the bird. Maybe it wasn't the classiest move ever, but no one had ever accused me of being a lady.

She hissed, and a string of very unpleasant suggestions of where I could shove certain things flew out of her mouth.

"Maybe later," I said, and kept right on walking...that is until I ran smack dab into Ida May. My ghost, who I'd only ever seen in spirit form, was standing in front of me, completely solid—and very much alive.

CHAPTER 4

"There you are!" Ida May yelled over the growing noise volume. "Do you have any idea how hard it is to find someone when you never pay attention to what they actually say? I mean, I knew you were riding on one of the floats, but I had no idea which one since there was less than a virgin's chance at an orgasm that I'd have ended up like this." She squealed and spun around, showing off her black sheer dress—make that *my* dress. "Like my outfit?"

So many questions ran through my mind, but I couldn't settle on anything other than, "What are you supposed to be?"

"You, of course. Can't you tell by the hair?" She was wearing a wig that was black on the top and bright purple on the bottom.

"Your hair looks nothing like mine." Mine was black with an electric blue streak on the side. Purple was not—and never would be—a color I'd choose for my hair, and I'd for damn certain never go for the ombre look. At least not with those colors.

"Close enough." She belted out a laugh. "Or just think of me as another slutty Bourbon Street babe."

"Hey." I scowled at her, inching to the right to let one of the brides by. "I'm not slutty."

"I know, but I am." She pumped her eyebrows a few times and scanned the crowd. Her gaze landed on a tall, clean-cut guy who was gaping at her. "I'm taking him home."

She started to lift her leg over the float's edge, but I clasped her around the wrist, stopping her. "First of all, he looks like he's barely eighteen years old. And you're—"

"Old enough to teach him a few things," she stated, her chest pushed forward with pride.

"Old enough to be his great, great, great—"

"That's enough. I get your point. He's legal; that's all that matters."

"Puh-lease… you don't know that. He could—" I stopped abruptly and shook my head, waving at her. "Ida May, how in the world did this happen?"

"The dress? I know where your spare keys are. I figured you wouldn't mind if I borrowed a few things, considering we're such good friends and all."

"A few things?" I scanned her body, noting she was also wearing my matching black lace bra and panties. "Ida May! Dammit." I pressed my hand to my forehead and took a deep breath. The clothes didn't matter… much. The dress was vintage and pretty expensive, but that was hardly the issue at the moment. "I didn't mean the dress. I meant you. How come you're not a ghost?"

She shrugged. "No idea. One minute, I was floating around; the next, I was standing on the counter in the café with a piece of chalk in my hand."

"Chalk?"

She grinned. "I was inspired."

Lord. What was I going to find when I walked into the café the next day? Ida May made a habit of dreaming up inappropriate menu items and adding crass jokes to our menu.

"You just suddenly appeared in solid form?" I asked, my eyes narrowed in suspicion. There were plenty of witches around town. I'd never heard of a spell that brought ghosts back from the dead. At least not ones that weren't incredibly complicated and dealt with black magic. "No one came in the store? No spells were cast? No magic beans?"

"Nope. Nothing. But I'm not complaining. Look at these." She palmed her ample breasts. "Real-live flesh, and by the end of the night, I'm going to have some young gorgeous thing suckling—"

"Stop!" I held up my hand. "Don't say anything else."

"Fine. Fine. For someone who owns a sheer dress, you sure are a prude." She grabbed a bag of beads from Vale, who was walking by, tossed her two-toned hair over her shoulder, and yelled, "Who wants to show me their tits?"

"Classy," Vale said.

"That's Ida May." I reluctantly positioned myself beside her if for no other reason than to keep an eye on her. Going from ghost to human wasn't something that just happened. Dark forces could have been at play. I pulled my phone out of my skirt pocket, and because the noise was starting to overwhelm me, instead of calling, I sent Julius a text.

Ida May somehow turned human. Send reinforcements.

I thought about texting Jade—my friend and leader of the New Orleans coven—a message, as well, but she was busy dealing with a new baby. Unless something dire happened, I didn't want to bother her.

He texted right back. *What?*

She showed up on my float in human form, and now she's tossing beads out to people who show her their breasts.

It took a moment, and I imagined Julius shaking his head in exasperation before sending his response. *Stay with her. I'm tied up at the moment, but will be there as soon as possible. If anything at all strange... err frightening happens, call me ASAP.*

Will do.

I put the phone on vibrate and tucked it away.

Ida May was busy having the time of her life, dangling beads and bantering with random strangers as the float rolled on. I stood in the middle of the chaos, taking it all in. Vampire bride hopefuls were drinking hurricanes from oversized glasses. Vale and another young man were weaving their way through the women, making sure everyone had beads or stuffed vampires to throw. And up at the top, near the cake, were Carver and Marcella sparring, just as they'd said they would.

Their movements were precise. Graceful. Everything about each of them screamed power and strength. They matched each other blow for blow, each anticipating the other's moves. Not once did either get a clean strike. There was something about their technique I couldn't put my finger on.

It was too perfect. Too calculated.

Too... supernatural.

CHAPTER 5

*W*ere they witches? I squinted up at Carver. It was possible. Sex witches maybe. That would explain why they were both so beautiful.

Vale brushed past me and then stopped suddenly. "Is something wrong, Pyper?"

"Why?" I narrowed my eyes at him, suspicious. He was part of Carver's inner circle.

"Nothing. You just seem like you're not having any fun. Can I get you anything? A hurricane? Or Champagne?"

"Oh, no." I waved a hand, feeling foolish. This guy was just a college student making some extra cash. Nothing odd about him at all. "Thanks, but I'm the designated keeper tonight." I cast a glance at Ida May. "Someone needs to make sure she stays out of trouble."

He laughed and tilted his head toward Carver and Marcella. "I know the feeling."

The two sparring above us didn't seem quite as perfect as they had before in their movements. Marcella slipped and stumbled to the right, which threw Carver off his next blow, and he lunged forward, unable to stop his momentum. Both paused the fight and started to laugh at something Marcella had said.

"They seem like they're enjoying themselves," I said, wondering if I'd let my imagination get the better of me earlier.

"They were overdue." Vale eyed them with a quiet smile, the kind usually reserved for those one's closest to.

Carver turned to the crowd. "It's important that my bride likes to have fun, and I think judging by the party we've managed to throw, that you've all passed that test."

"Damn straight! And I've got incriminating photos to prove it," a woman said from behind me.

The speaker once again was the redhead. She had a pile of beads around her neck and nothing else. Her top was gone, and while the beads covered most of her chest, one nipple was peeking out from between the strands.

Lord. Someone needed to take away her drinking privileges.

"But there's more to being a vampire bride than just having fun," Carver continued. "Vampires have a long history of being hunted. Therefore, it's important you all know how to fight. Marcella and I just put on a demonstration. Now it's your turn. Only the fiercest will be considered. I don't want to meet the love of my life, and then be left a widower when she can't avoid a stake. That would be tragic." He placed his hand over his heart and turned puppy-dog eyes on the crowd.

It worked like a charm. A collective *awww* went up among the women.

I rolled my eyes.

Vale chuckled. "You're not buying any of his bullshit, are you?"

"He is laying it on pretty thick."

"It's just part of the show. If Carver's smart, he'll pick you."

I shook my head. "I'm taken."

Vale shrugged. "Who cares? So is he."

"Really?" That was news. He was an outrageous flirt, but then so was I… usually.

"Sure. You didn't know he's with Marcella?"

I snapped my attention back to the pair now each sparring with some of the bride hopefuls. "No wonder they look magical when they're together."

Vale turned his head and studied me. "What do you mean 'magical'?"

"There's just something about the way they move. When they were sparring, it was almost too perfect. Ethereal. You know?" I eyed a tray of hurricanes one of the women carried as it went by, and I immediately regretted my resolve to stay focused on Ida May. A drink was pretty much exactly what I needed at that moment. "Have they been together a long time?"

"Longer than most," he said and passed his last bag of stuffed vampires off to one of the riders. "Years. But like I said, they don't see each other often. Marcella is usually… away for long stretches of time."

"That's rough. I had a long-distance relationship once, but being apart didn't work for us. I know Carver's busy building up his club. What does Marcella do?" She was so elegant in her costume, it was hard to imagine her working a regular job at all. I pictured her sipping sweet tea on the veranda while discussing which charity gala to attend.

He shrugged. "Mostly, she spends her time planning things." He gestured to the float. "The wedding was her idea."

"Really?" An event planner who was always out of town? Maybe her business was rooted in another city. Plus, Carver was sort of new in town. "Seems like with what they both do, it shouldn't be too hard for one of them to relocate."

He snorted out a laugh. "They're working on it." Then he jerked his head toward Carver and Marcella. "Ready to spar?"

"Oh, I don't think so. I'm not interested in winning a date with Carver." My fingers inched to check my phone to see if Julius had texted, but it was set to vibrate, and I hadn't felt anything.

"Date?" He laughed. "If you think Marcella is going to let him spend any time with the chosen one, well… think again. Na, this is just about putting on a show, and the ones up there right now are failing. Badly."

Carver was currently sidestepping Morticia and staring at her with disgust. Her sporadic moves resembled someone having a seizure. The only way she'd be able to land a blow was by pure luck. If fighting was a requirement, she'd just been disqualified.

I glanced over at Ida May. She was working her way through two bags of throws with one inappropriate comment after another. "Oh, honey. You know they have silicone these days, right?" and "Have you considered phalloplasty? It might help you get your confidence back."

I would have died from embarrassment back at the café, but here, on the float in the middle of a parade, she was in her element. There seemed no real reason to babysit her, except for that pesky fact that she'd turned human. I leaned in behind her and said, "Stay here, okay? I'm going to go talk to Carver."

"Pfft. I'm not going anywhere. Not as long as the throws and hurricanes hold out, anyway."

Judging by the pile of beads at her feet and the giant three-foot-tall plastic hurricane glass in her hand, there was no chance of her jumping ship anytime soon. "Okay, then. I'll be back. Try to behave."

She twisted and gave me a horrified look. "You've got to be kidding me. It's Halloween. And I've been dead for decades. Behaving isn't on my agenda."

I bit back a laugh. "Fair enough. Just don't wander off anywhere without me."

She waved a dismissive hand and went back to entertaining the crowds.

"Lead on," I said to Vale.

He waved a hand. "After you."

CHAPTER 6

"You need to choose Pyper," Vale said to Carver.

I stood next to Vale and his uncle as the three of us watched Marcella continue to spar with the redhead.

"What makes you think that?" Carver asked, curiosity in his tone.

"Just trust me," he said.

"Die, bitch," Redhead cried and brandished a silver spike, lunging at Marcella, barely missing her shoulder.

I gasped. What the hell was she doing? This was make-believe, not *Buffy the Vampire Slayer.*

An ugly scowl claimed Marcella's face. In one quick movement, she seized Redhead's wrist and plucked the spike from her hand. Then she spun the girl around and caught her in a chokehold. "Never speak to me that way again. Got it?"

I watched, my eyes widening at the fierceness in Marcella's tone.

"I'm just playing the game," Redhead squeaked.

"Respect. Learn it." Marcella released her and stood there fuming as her eyes shifted from black to brilliant blue and then back again.

"Whoa," I said to Carver. "How'd she do that?"

"She's very skilled at fighting. That move was pretty basic, actually."

"No, not that. Her eyes. Does she have some sort of special contacts? I'd be all over those for the gallery shows I do." I had recently begun selling prints of my body-painted models. At the shows, I usually had a few painted people milling about to show off my work.

"That's what I was talking about," Vale said to Carver. "She sees things. That makes her a worthy pick."

I frowned at them. "What are you talking about?"

Carver's lips turned up into a slow smile. "Are you a seer?"

I shook my head. "No. I'm more of a medium."

"You can talk to ghosts then?" Carver asked, interest sparkling in his eyes.

"Yes." I sighed, wishing I was anywhere but trapped on the float. It wasn't that it bothered me to talk about my ability—I just hated when people started asking questions about those they'd lost. My gift didn't work that way.

"It bothers you to talk about it?" Carver asked.

"No. I was just hoping for a night off," I said, forcing a smile.

"We're not asking you to contact anyone," Carver said. "Tonight would be useless anyway. Too much chaos. But you are *very* interesting." He clamped his hand on Vale's back. "You're right. I think we've made our decision, but it's best if we at least go through the motions of sparring."

"I don't think—"

Carver wrapped his freezing hand around my wrist and pulled me into the middle of the platform. "Come on, gorgeous. Let's see what you've got."

And before I could protest again, he reached for me with lightning speed. My defense training kicked in, and I spun, catching his arm with both hands, and then yanked it back as hard as I could.

A voice in the back of my mind kept protesting, warning me that this was just a show. We were on a float in the middle of the parade, people partying all around us. But I ignored it. This felt real.

Carver twisted and easily freed himself from my grasp, and in the next instant, his leg kicked out, knocking me on my ass. I rolled, coming up on my feet, ready for more.

Carver grinned, showing those fangs again. A chill ran up my spine. The campiness had disappeared and moved straight into one hundred percent creepy. He feigned right, then left and when I miscalculated by going for a blow to his gut and missed, he grabbed my wrist and twisted me until my back was flush against his chest. He held me in a death grip and dipped his head down to my neck, his cold-ass breath making me feel sick to my stomach.

"Hey!" Ida May called. "Get off her. Just because everyone else on this float wants to throw their panties at you doesn't mean Pyper is that kind of girl."

I glanced up, finding Ida May, steamrolling straight for us.

"She's right, you know," I said. "I'm not the panty-throwing kind of girl."

"Why do you think I want you so much?" he whispered. "It's been about a century since I've had a really good challenge."

"Cut it out, Saint. This vampire shtick is getting really old." My patience had long since disappeared, and his act was really pissing me off.

A laugh rumbled up from the back of his throat. "You really don't get it, do you—oomph!"

We both jerked forward from a sudden impact, and if Carver hadn't been hanging on to me, I was certain I'd have face-planted. Instead, Carver regained his balance and steadied me, never once letting go.

"I said, get off her." Ida May stood off to the side, holding a bag of beads. "Or do you want me to smack you in the head this time?"

Her eyes were narrowed and full of venom. It was an expression I'd never seen on her before.

Marcella stepped up beside her, laughing to herself. "You two are perfect."

"Excuse me." I felt Carver's grip on me relax, and without another thought, I jabbed my elbow as hard as I could into his gut.

He grunted and released me. I was certain it was more from shock than strength, but that was all I'd been going for anyway.

Ida May grabbed my hand and tugged me to her side. "We'll be leaving now," she told Carver. "No one manhandles my friend like that."

"Neither of you are going anywhere." Marcella snapped her fingers, and suddenly, all the wannabe brides froze in place... everyone except for Ida May and me.

My ghostly friend stilled and looked around in confusion while the parade goers let out gasps of delighted surprise. She glared at Marcella. "What the bloody hell are you up to?"

"You, Ms. Ida May, and your friend Pyper here are the

two lovely women who've been picked to be Carver's brides," Marcella said with a saccharine-sweet smile.

"What? No," I cried.

"Two brides? I'm not going to be anyone's sister wife. You've lost your dammed mind if you think I'm going to share." Ida May fisted her hands on her hips and fixed them both with a deranged stare.

"Ida May," I whispered. "We're supposed to be leaving, remember?"

"Right, right. Sorry. They distracted me with their crazy." She turned back to Carver. "We're leaving. Find some other suckers to marry."

"That's not going to happen." Marcella nodded to Vale, who moved to stand in front of the makeshift stairs, blocking our exit. "You two are the most entertaining. And above all, the show must go on."

I took a step back, prepared to jump off this freak show, but Carver wrapped his hands around my arms, stopping me. His hands were ice cold, and I shivered as he whispered, "Where're you going, my friend?"

"Let go," I demanded, my flight instinct kicking in. There was something seriously off about all three of them. I'd brushed it off as Halloween costumes and shenanigans, but that didn't explain Marcella's crazy color-flashing eyes, Carver's ice-cold touch, or the bloody fangs I'd seen after Marcella had appeared to bite that stranger from the crowd.

Even though everything was supposed to be a show, there was no denying all signs pointed to *vampire*—real, cold-blooded, neck-biting, blood-sucking fiends.

My world spun slightly as I imagined myself in some weird alternate reality. Were Carver, Vale, and Marcella really vamps? Was all of this for real?

No. That was crazy. Vampires didn't exist. Witches, demons, angels, even incubi. But vampires? Surely if that were the case, I'd have known that by now. Wouldn't I?

No.

The voice was the one in the back of my head that knew better. I'd seen far too much over the last few years. Time to call in the cavalry. I whipped out my phone and was two lines into a group text to Julius and every other witch and incubus I knew when Carver grabbed the phone out of my hand, threw it on the ground, and crushed it with his ugly-ass boot.

"Hey! You bastard." I slugged him in the chest and winced at the hard impact. "Ouch. Son of a bitch. You owe me for that. Do you know how much iPhones cost?"

Carver gripped the back of my neck and squeezed. "You don't need a phone for the foreseeable future," he said in a quiet conversational tone, though his hand was digging into my flesh so hard, I got the feeling if I moved, he'd snap me in two. "Now relax. Protesting is only going to make things worse for Ida May."

What the hell did that mean? Worse for Ida May?

The ghost in question was fighting Vale's hold as he piled her hair on the top of her head while Marcella waited with an antique veil.

"You two are going to pay. I know people! Powerful witches and demon hunters. Get off me," she demanded, but neither paid her any mind.

Marcella jabbed the haircomb into Ida May's bun with so much force, Ida May flinched.

"Watch it, would ya? Damn." She lifted her hand and rubbed at the spot on her head. "I think you might have drawn blood."

The ugly scowl on Marcella's face made me wonder why I'd ever thought she was so beautiful. She snapped her fingers again, and the rest of the women on the float came to life, each resuming their activities without ever missing a beat.

Carver leaned down and said, "Relax. It's just a party. In a few minutes, you and Ida May will be the stars of the show."

Just a party. Right. That's why he smashed my phone. Uh huh. A ritual is what Marcella had said. But for what? I turned, eyeing Vale, who was still blocking the stairs. The only way off this horror trap was if I wanted to fling myself over the side. I might've resorted to that if it hadn't been for Ida May.

Carver, still clutching my neck, dragged me over to where Ida May stood in the middle of the platform. Her moth-eaten veil made her look as though she'd just climbed out of a tomb.

"Can you believe this?" she asked me, waving a hand at the offending piece of lace. "Don't they know how to preserve anything?"

"Does it matter?" I asked her.

"Of course it does. It's hideous. Even if this is a forced, vampire-harem wedding, I still want to look good."

The float came to a stop in the middle of Canal Street, the place the wedding and blood ritual was supposed to happen.

Carver released me, but I felt rather than saw both Vale and Marcella step up behind us. It was pretty clear that if I so much as moved a muscle, the shit was going to hit the fan.

"Ladies!" Carver said into a cordless microphone. "Thank you. It's been a wonderful night, but now it's time to claim my bride... or *brides* as the fates may have it."

A loud roar of surprise rose from the crowd.

"It turns out I can't make up my mind." He lifted Ida May's hand in the air and gave her a slight bow. Despite the dirty look she cast in his direction, when she turned to the crowd, she flushed, and her eyes brightened with excitement. After being visible to only me for however many months, she was finally getting her moment in the spotlight.

Too bad I was pretty certain we were both going to be vamp food in a few minutes. I glanced around, desperately searching for Julius. But the massive sea of people crowded around the floats made spotting anyone impossible. I had to do something. But what?

I had no phone and no real hope of escaping the float unscathed, though I'd certainly try. My only weapons were the heels on my boots, and… oh! The stake I'd shoved in my bootleg as part of my costume.

A shudder ran through me. Was I really contemplating staking someone? If I had to, I would.

"Isn't she lovely?" Carver asked the crowd. The partygoers cheered him on, drowning out the jeers of the ladies on the float. Then he turned to me and waved a hand. "My other bride is also this lovely lady, Pyper. Tonight, I make them both mine. Forever."

Ida May turned into him and, with a sly smile, ran her fingers down his chest suggestively. "I'm all you really need, gorgeous."

I rolled my eyes. Leave it to Ida May to ham it up even when she knew everything was one step away from disaster. But then if I'd been dead for almost a hundred years, maybe I would to.

"But before we can get to the ceremony, we must complete the blood ritual to satisfy the offering to our elders." Carver grinned, showing off those sharp fangs as he first glanced at Marcella and then lowered his head and made a show of scraping his teeth down Ida May's neck.

Ida May stiffened, and fear shone back at me as she met my gaze.

"Together!" Marcella ordered.

Vale grabbed my torso, his viselike grip knocking the wind out of me, but it didn't stop me from flailing my arms and legs. Just as we got to Carver's side, my foot connected, and Vale let out a loud grunt as we both fell into a heap on the floor of the float.

"Dammit," he gasped out, holding his crotch. "Son of a bitch."

I scrambled to my feet, and while everyone was still focused on the writhing vamp, I grabbed my stake from my boot and palmed it.

"Looks like my other bride's a little feisty," Carver said into the microphone.

"Feisty?" I said. "More like pissed as hell."

Vale let out a low hiss, and then a second later, he grabbed my booted foot, anchoring me in place.

"Get off." I tried to kick out, but got nowhere.

Vale rose slowly to his feet, his eyes flashing that brilliant blue, the same as Marcella's had.

"Enough!" Marcella said. "Just complete the ritual."

Vale lifted me off my feet and snarled as he went straight for my neck. My heart thundered in my ears, and my palm was sweaty on my stake. But I was prepared, already going for the vampire's heart.

But just before Vale tore into my flesh, Marcella cried, "No!" and flew in between us. The stake landed in her shoulder, surprising both of us.

"You bitch," she spat and tore the wood from her flesh.

Pale-pink liquid oozed down her arm and over her black-and-silver dress. Definitely not human. Carver and Vale were both cursing, while Ida May, for once in her life, remained quiet.

"Pyper," I heard her call, but I couldn't tear my eyes from Marcella. Tears shone in her eyes as she stared at her now-clawed hand, still holding the stake.

The chestnut-haired woman's words from earlier in the evening came flooding back. *Beware of the one with claws.*

CHAPTER 7

"*C*arver! Time's almost up," Marcella said, her eyes frantic.

He glanced at her, pain and desperation lining his normally handsome face. Then he scowled, and his fangs descended, turning him into a true monster.

Ida May backed up, pressing against the railing of the float. But he was on her too fast, a true predator going after his prey.

"No!" I started to move toward them, but Vale grabbed me around the waist and yanked me back. I flailed, kicking my feet back as hard as I could. "Get the hell off me!"

Ida May let out a blood-curdling scream, but it cut off suddenly as if she'd been silenced.

"Your turn," Vale said, undisturbed by my attempts to free myself. But before he could go in for the kill, Morticia and Redhair jumped him. The shock of their attack took him down in a heap.

"You bastards," Redhair cried. "I can't believe you chose those two over us."

"Yeah, they're nothing special. No guts at all," Morticia added as the pair of them continued to try to gain control of Vale.

Christ. Those two really were crazy.

The urge to flee hit me, but I couldn't leave without knowing what had happened to Ida May. I skirted around the trio still wrestling on the floor and spotted Marcella. She was slumped in a chair, appearing barely conscious, with the stake resting at her feet.

I grabbed for it and cried out when her claw tangled in my hair and pulled me up.

"You bitch, you nearly ruined everything." Her lips were twisted with an evil sneer. "As soon as Carver drains her, I'll be brought back to this world, and then you're next."

Rage rose from the depths of my soul. Whatever she was —vampire, demon, or troll—I didn't care. She was done.

"What are you going to do now, Pyper Rayne?" She yanked on my hair, contorting my back until the agony of it made my vision blur.

"This!" I yelled, and with a force I didn't know I possessed, I reared up, ignoring the intense pain searing through my neck and spine, and slammed the stake into her chest.

Her mouth formed into a shocked O as she froze. Then a light crackled through her body, lighting her up from the inside out until she finally exploded into a heap of sand.

Everything around us stopped. I heard nothing—only saw the tiny speckles of earth that used to be Marcella.

"Holy shit," I heard Redhair say beside me.

I cut my gaze to her. She and Morticia were standing over Vale, who was curled into a ball, rocking back and forth as if he were a mental patient.

"I think we should get out of here," Morticia said to Redhair.

"Good plan," I shot back as they scrambled down the stairs.

Across the stage, Carver was holding Ida May in his arms, his expression full of frantic concern. "We have to get her to the hospital. She's been hurt!"

"Stop right there!" Julius came running up the stairs, his dark, wavy hair flying out from behind him. He twisted and turned, magic crackling at his fingertips, no doubt searching for any form of threat.

"She needs help," Carver said again.

I climbed to my feet, intensely grateful Julius had arrived, even if he was five seconds too late.

He spotted me and ran over.

I pointed to Ida May. "You need to help her."

"What happened?" he asked as he took her from Carver.

"I don't know," Carver said, his brow furrowed. "The last thing I remember was walking onto the float with Pyper. The next thing I know, I've got this woman in my arms, and she's unconscious."

"Not just unconscious," I barked. "Bleeding."

"What? Where?" he asked, scanning her body.

"Right there!" I pointed to her neck and then gasped as I realized she wasn't bleeding at all. But I had seen Carver bite her. He even still had red stains around his mouth.

"It's the ritual," the chestnut-haired woman said, floating up the stairs.

I backed up. "Who are you?"

Julius glanced over at her, frowning. "Bella, what are you doing here?"

"Keeping an eye on those from the otherworld." She met my gaze. "You made my night a lot easier. Thank you."

"Easier? Are you kidding me? People almost died."

"And some almost got a new lease on life. Thanks to you, Marcella and her followers didn't." She waved to the other side of the float, the one that had contained the women Marcella had arrived with. It was empty.

"They're gone," I said, unable to wrap my head around what had happened.

"When you neutralized Marcella, they lost their connection to this world." She glanced at Julius and Ida May. "Your friend will reawaken in a few minutes. It was nice seeing you again, Julius. Have a good year."

No one said a word as we watched her fade away into the ether.

Ida May's eyes popped open. She took one look at Carver and jumped out of Julius's arms, screaming bloody murder. "You ugly piece of stank vampire trash. How dare you try to kill me? Do you have any idea what it's like to go through life dead?"

Carver held up his hands and took a step back. "Whoa. I don't have any idea what you're talking about."

Vale, who'd finally gotten to his feet, rubbed a hand down his face and shook his head. "How did I get here? I thought I was supposed to be on the zombie float."

I stared at Julius, helpless. "I have no idea what's going on."

"I do." He wrapped an arm around my waist. "Let's get out of here."

"Yeah. Let's go. This float sucks," Ida May added.

"Give me just a sec." Julius walked over to Carver and

Vale, spoke to them for a moment, then shook each of their hands, sending a tiny spark of magic zipping into them.

"Memory spell?" I asked Julius when he rejoined me.

He nodded. "They were victims of Marcella. All I did was give them a few memories of the night, so they don't think they blacked out. The float will continue on to the end, but we're out of here."

I let him lead me off the float and into the happy crowd. They cheered for me and Ida May, praising our acting and asking for an encore.

I shook my head, but Ida May was swept up in the attention and said, "I'm riding this pony for as long as it lasts. Don't wait up."

"Here." I gave her my tickets to the Night of the Living Dead Ball. "One is for you, and one is for Nissa. She's on the Daiquiri Dolls float."

"Oh, an after-party. You know how much trouble I can get into at one of those?" Her eyes sparkled with glee.

"Yes. Do whatever you want, but don't ditch Nissa. I promised her a ticket."

"Would I do that?" She smirked and disappeared back into the parade route, to continue entertaining her fans.

"Want to explain everything that went on back there?" I asked Julius once we made our way onto one of the side streets away from the festivities.

He took a deep breath. "I had my suspicions when I saw you stake that wannabe vampire, but I didn't know for sure until Bella showed up. She's a goddess of the damned. And Marcella, the one you staked? Is that the name she was using?"

I nodded.

"She's one of Bella's charges. She fancies herself a

vampire, but really, she's a ghost with a damned soul. Tonight, Halloween night, is the only one where she has any power to materialize. Looks like she formed a plan to do just that. But there are sacrifices and rituals involved. Everything from possession to soul transfers. If she'd been successful, she'd have risen again, but since you stopped her, she'll be out of commission for decades, if not more."

I leaned into him, enjoying his warmth. "And what about Carver and Vale? What are they?"

"Human. She used a soul possession on them to get them to do what she wanted."

"That doesn't explain the teeth or Carver's ice-cold body temperature."

Julius cast me a suspicious glance. "His body temperature?"

"Please." I sighed and shook my head. "He kept trying to manhandle me. I couldn't help but notice."

"Sorry," he said gently and kissed the top of my head. "It's all part of her illusion. Carver was never really any of those things."

I found that hard to believe. I'd seen him bite Ida May. Or had I? She hadn't had one mark on her neck after he'd broken free of the spell.

"And Ida May? Why is she in human form? Do you know?" I asked him, deciding I didn't care about Marcella or whatever whacked-out spells she was using. As long as she was gone, that was all that mattered.

He smiled. "All Soul's Night. She's become human because it's what she wants most. And she likely went looking for you because you're the one person on this earth she has a connection to. By midnight, she'll be in ghost form again."

"That's sad," I said, unlocking the door to my apartment building.

Julius followed me in. "Which part?"

"The part where she'll turn ghostly again. She's so full of life. You should've seen her." I laughed. "My goodness, she's out of control."

"When isn't she?" He followed me up the stairs and held my apartment door open for me.

"Good point."

He closed the door and reached out, gently taking my hand in his. "Are you okay?"

His voice was barely a whisper, but it reached that place deep in the middle of my chest, warming me from the inside out.

I turned into him, reveling in the heat of his skin against mine. The events of the night washed away, and all I wanted was to get lost in him. "Yeah. I think so. But you know what will make me even better?"

He glanced at the bedroom. "Flannel pajamas and a hot cocoa?"

"Try again," I said, unbuttoning his shirt.

"Hot bath and a glass of wine?"

"Nope." I pushed his shirt off his shoulders and trailed my lips across his shoulder.

He sucked in a sharp breath. "Oh, I see, now. Hot sex with your favorite witch?"

"As long as he's off duty." I rose onto my toes and brushed my lips over his. "Interruptions aren't part of my plan."

He yanked me to him and ran his hand along my upper thigh, only stopping when he cupped my backside. His eyes sparked with heat as he said, "No interruptions. At least not until midnight, when a certain ghost shows up, complaining... loudly."

I chuckled and glanced over at the clock. "That leaves an hour and twenty-two minutes. You up for the challenge?"

Julius brought his lips to mine and whispered, "Always."

KISSED BY TEMPTATION

The last place sex-witch Mati Ballintine wants to be is at a holiday sorority party. But when the high angel from the council orders her to protect a new angel recruit, she has no choice but to go and grit her teeth through the frat boys' advances.

The night turns from bad to worse when a demon appears and is hell-bent on taking the angel to Hell. Mati and her incubus boyfriend Vaughn will need to combine forces to not only save the angel, but everyone else the demon leaves in his wake.

CHAPTER 1

*G*oing to school full time while keeping an eye on some newbie angel sucked ass. Especially when the new recruit was raiding my closet for a dress that wouldn't make her look like she was fresh off the buggy from Amish country.

"Oh, my," Janie said, a blush creeping up her pale flesh. "This one, um... looks like it's missing a couple of yards of fabric."

I glanced at the silk spaghetti-strap dress and sent her a sly smile. "It gets the job done."

"Only if you're looking to..." She bit her lip as heat nearly radiated off her bright red cheeks.

I held back a snarky remark. Damn my sister Chessandra for foisting the newbie angel on me. Chessandra was the high angel of the angel council, and lucky me, every time she had a pet project, she tapped me to do it. And I wasn't even an angel—I was a witch. A sex witch, at that. Not exactly the most respectable of witches in the eyes of the public. But that was their problem, not mine. I found it empowering, and, let's face it, fun.

But it also meant most of my wardrobe had been purchased specifically for seduction. If Janie was going to shop in my closet, she was going to look hot by the time I was done with her. "Try this one," I said, handing her a silk dress with a plunging halter-top neckline.

"I don't—"

"If you wear that dress you've got on"—I swept my skeptical gaze down the length of her body—"you're going to stick out like a church lady at a wet-T-shirt contest."

"Mati!" She grabbed the halter and pressed it against her chest. "If I wear this, I might as well head straight for the strip bar. There's no way this... handkerchief is going to cover all this." Arching her back, she waved a hand in front of her ample chest.

I refrained from rolling my eyes. "Just try it on."

She ran a hand through her perfectly coiled curls, unintentionally turning her look from too perfect to casually mussed. It was a start. She bit her lower lip. "I'm not sure about this."

"Janie..." I gave her a stern look.

She swallowed, closed her eyes, and disappeared into my bathroom.

I let out a long sigh. Janie was a sweet girl, and I genuinely liked her. I just wasn't a big fan of the night's planned activity. We were headed to a holiday party put on by her sorority at the university, an elite Greek house only for those with magical gifts. It was hard to imagine she'd even want to be a part of the group considering she seemed happier in the book club and the drama department. That is until I met her mother—a socialite witch from Memphis whose life revolved around people of a certain social status and their connections. Janie was a legacy recruit, and if she hadn't joined, her mom would've made her life hell.

Which was ironic, considering Janie was a low-level angel who would spend her life protecting souls from demons. She'd literally have her fair share of run-ins with Hell. In fact, it had already started. A week ago, Janie had accidently crossed paths with a couple of demons and barely escaped. It was now my job to keep her safe while the other resident New Orleans angel, Lailah, tracked the demons down.

I stared at my closet, contemplating the night's outfit. If Vaughn were in town, I'd wear the silver-beaded number with the slit up to my hip just to torture him until we could get somewhere private. Oh, why not? It'd been weeks since I'd felt sexy. I pulled the dress out and slipped it on. The bodice showed just enough cleavage to be enticing but was still tasteful, while the skirt hit mid-thigh, showing off ample leg. It was that slit that put the dress into the danger zone. And I loved it.

The door to the bathroom swung open slowly. Janie's blond head poked around the corner, a grimace on her face. "This isn't going to work."

"Get your skinny ass out here," I said as I slipped into my matching silver heels.

Her eyes widened as she took in my transformation.

"Janie." I stood with my hands on my hips. "You're going to be late."

She glanced at my wall clock, and then with a pained expression, she shuffled out of the bathroom. Her arms were crossed over her chest, hiding the deep plunge showing off her magnificent breasts. Damn, what I wouldn't have given for a pair of those double Ds.

I grinned at her. "It's perfect. Classy with just a little bit of sin."

"A little?" She patted at her curls. "I messed up my hair."

"No you didn't." I reached over and mussed them just a little more. "Perfect. Now slip on those shoes and we'll get out of here."

She strapped her feet into the black kitten heels I'd put out for her. Her scowl vanished as she admired them and seemed to relax a tiny bit. They were a far cry from my four-inch stilettos. Still, she couldn't seem to keep from wrapping her arms around herself in an attempt to keep her cleavage covered.

"Here." I handed her a loosely knitted sweater that would give her a layer of fabric but not really cover anything. "Stand up straight and stop fidgeting. There's nothing more attractive than a girl with confidence. Got it?"

Her arms fell to her sides as she forced a smile and trailed after me as if she were on a death march.

"Janie?"

"Yeah." Her fists clenched, but at least she didn't cover her chest again.

"Do you want me to get you out of this? I can come up with something."

She pressed her lips together, clearly in thought, and then shook her head. "No. Thank you, but I'm supposed to be meeting someone there. I don't want to disappoint him. Otherwise, I might take you up on the offer. This sort of thing just isn't my scene, you know?"

I nodded. I did know. It used to be my kind of scene, but only because hot, horny college guys would be there and they were easy pickings. These days, I steered clear. Who needed frat guys when I had Vaughn, the hottest incubus demon hunter in town? "Who are you meeting? Anyone I need to check out first?"

A tinge of blush crept up her cheeks again. "No. He's just an athlete I tutored last semester. His aunt is a witch, so he knows about our world but doesn't have any power. He's not a threat in any way. We were supposed to bring dates, and well, he's a friend."

"Okay. Well then." I winked, determined to hook her up with jock boy. If anyone needed a night with a hot-blooded male, it was her. Grabbing my clutch purse, I said, "Let's go get 'em."

CHAPTER 2

*J*anie and I stood out front of the sorority house, staring at the twinkling snowflake lights. Each one was completely different and seemed to float in the air over the immaculate gardens.

"Gorgeous," I said.

Janie nodded. "They've been working for days on the decorations."

"It shows." Everything about the place was a magical winter wonderland. Isolated blue-silver snow fell and gathered on the window frames, leaving a frost on the glass despite the fifty-two-degree weather, and the doors and windows were draped with frosted garland blooming with live poinsettia flowers.

The air tasted of powerful magic, electrifying me. My pulse quickened and that desire that lived deep inside me rushed to the surface. Dammit, where was Vaughn when I needed him?

He'd been out of town the past three weeks, tracking a demon, and uh... without his attention, my power wasn't exactly up to par. Unfortunate for me, considering I had to go into the party full of supernaturals and protect Janie if a demon showed up. If anything went down, I was going to be seriously handicapped in the kick-ass-magic department.

If I'd had a choice, I would've gone straight home, popped the top on a fresh carton of Blue Bell ice cream, and had a Netflix marathon. Because in my current state, my sex-witch pheromones were going to be damned hard to keep under wraps.

Janie visibly shivered beside me in the chilly New Orleans air. "Ready?" she asked, her teeth chattering.

It wasn't that cold was it? That was one thing about being a sex witch, our blood ran a little warmer. "Sure." I waved a hand for her to go ahead of me.

As soon as Janie stepped into the yard, actual magical snowflakes started to drift from the sky. I couldn't help the tiny giggle that escaped when one hit my arm, causing magic to spark over my skin. "Nice touch."

Janie shook her arms, brushing the glowing flakes to the ground. "I don't like it. The magic stings a little."

"Really? That's unusual."

She shrugged. "It always has. Just one of my quirks, I guess." She said it in a mocking tone, making me believe that was something she'd heard a majority of her life. My heart cracked a bit at the thought. Then I was just pissed. This girl was gorgeous and smart, and I was getting the impression she hadn't heard that nearly enough.

I clasped my fingers around hers. "Come on. Let's go show you off and find that boy of yours."

A small smile curled her lips as she inclined her head and followed me up the glowing walkway.

"Welcome to a Kiss of Magic," the bubbly witch at the

door said, waving us in. "Here are your party favors. Please put them on then make your way to the champagne station. We're just about to start."

"About to start? I asked Janie.

"The meet and greet." The pained look on her face made me laugh.

"Okay. Don't worry, we'll do this together." While we stood waiting for our champagne flutes, I tore into the silver-wrapped box. Inside lay a snowflake-charm bracelet that glowed with power. It was warm to the touch and caused tingles to ripple across my skin. Oh, this would be fun if... never mind. No Vaughn, no tingles. I slipped the bracelet onto my wrist and tried to ignore the seductive magic building inside me.

"Oh," Janie said as she pulled out a snowflake pendant. It dangled on a silver chain. She held it up, peering at the snowflake but not touching it. Then with a sigh, she clasped it around her neck.

I frowned. "Are you going to be able to wear that? With magic being irritating to you and everything?"

She nodded. "I'll get used to it."

"No." I shook my head and ran my fingers lightly over her chest, forcing a small dose of magic to coat her skin.

"Hey!" She stepped back, her eyes wide and full of suspicion. "What did you do?"

I shrugged and grabbed the two glasses the bartender was holding out for us. "I just put a barrier between you and the charmed snowflake. So it won't bother you."

"But my chest is numb!"

"Better than irritated, right?"

"How did you know that wouldn't bother me as well?" She stood with her hands on her hips, staring me down.

Damn. She looked downright fierce with her eyes shooting daggers at me. She made me so proud.

I patted her hand. "Because it's a numbing spell. By definition you shouldn't feel it. Do you?"

"No..." She shuffled her feet. "But I feel... a little odd. Like, more alive or something."

Should I have told her it was my sex-witch energy? Nah. Better to let her figure it out for herself.

"It's just the party. The excitement in the air." I nodded toward the makeshift stage. "Looks like things are getting started."

A tall, sandy-haired, clean-cut guy appeared and slipped his arm around Janie's waist. She let out a small yelp as she jumped in surprise.

"Hey, it's just me, Janie." He smiled down at her and leaned in to kiss her on her cheek.

Just a friend? Sure. I hid a chuckle and turned away.

"Chad," she said breathlessly. "You made it."

The sexual tension radiating off the pair of them was enough to make gooseflesh pop out over my skin. Whoa. Those two had it bad. And in my sex-deprived state, their energy was driving me insane. I took another step to the right, putting more distance between us, only I bumped right into a bronze-skinned god of epic proportions.

"Excuse me," I said, glancing up into the clearest blue eyes I'd ever seen. They were hypnotizing. I was caught in his gaze, dumbfounded by their beauty. "Uh..."

He chuckled and stepped back, giving me a little space. "Hello there, Mati."

I stood completely still, trying to place him. My track record with men was pretty long. Before Vaughn, I was a love 'em and leave 'em kind of girl. Emotional attachments weren't my thing. So my list of sexual partners was longer than your average twenty-two-year-old. But this guy? This long, lean, corded guy of beauty? I'd have remembered him. "How did you know my name?"

He held his hand out. "I'm Chase. I work with Vaughn."

My eyebrows shot straight up. "And you're here because...?"

"Routine. Any place full of magical beings is a demon draw. The party is my assignment for the night."

"And Vaughn told you to look for me?"

He nodded. "I'm to be your date so no one else gets any ideas." His smile was easy and teasing.

Ideas weren't exactly the problem, but he was right. With him by my side, the men would think twice before getting grabby.

"Welcome to Wicca Delta Mu's Kiss of Magic holiday soiree!" A gorgeous redhead with bright green eyes stood on the stage holding a mic. "We're so excited you're all here to share our magical evening. And now it's time to get this party started!" Her arms flew in the air and the lights cut out, leaving us all in complete darkness.

There was a cry of excited surprise that shuddered through the room, followed immediately by candles lighting spontaneously on the tables and in the wall sconces. As my eyes adjusted, the first thing I noticed was that each and every woman was wearing a piece of snowflake jewelry that was pulsing with magic.

My body responded instantly, bringing my sexual energy right to the surface. And there was nothing I could do about it. The sex-witch pheromones filtered out into the crowd.

"What are you doing?" Chase scowled. "That's only going to make both of our jobs harder."

"I didn't do it on purpose," I said, not surprised he knew exactly what had happened. He was an incubus, for God's sake. "It was the sudden influx of magic." I pointed to my bracelet. "See?"

He studied the snowflake charms and then glanced around. "Can you feel it radiating off everyone?"

I nodded.

"That's damned inconvenient."

I shrugged. It was, but it was beyond my control.

"Now here's the fun part," Bubbly Girl said, grinning. "Every ten minutes, the candles will flicker, and that's the cue it's time to meet someone new. When your magical charms glow bright blue, that means you've found your dance partner for the dance-off."

"Oh son of a...," I mumbled as Chase chuckled.

"You don't dance?" Chase's eyes lit with amusement.

"Oh, I dance. I just prefer to pick my partner... and I don't compete."

He snorted. "Right."

I turned and cast a skeptical glance down the length of his body. Then I stared him dead in the eye. "Do I look like a girl who has a hard time getting what she wants?"

It was a bitchy thing to say. I had advantages other women didn't because of my powers, but damn it if this sorority mixer wasn't annoying. Whatever happened to throwing a party, supplying booze, and letting everyone drink themselves into a good time?

Chase just laughed. "I guess not."

I glanced over at Janie. She had her hand on Chad's chest and was smiling up at him. The look of adoration on his face had me relaxing. Okay, for Janie I could mingle with the frat boys. No big deal.

Chase was lured away by a sexy little number with wildflower tattoos covering her shoulder. Two other girls flocked to the pair almost immediately. Yeah, incubi had the same gift... or curse... that I did. He'd be occupied for the foreseeable future.

I turned to the guy on my left, resigned to the fact if I was going to appear to be one of the crowd, I was going to have to participate. "Hi," I said. "So are you—"

"Damn, baby," he said, practically ripping my dress off with his gaze. "You're the hottest fucking chick in this place."

"Well, wasn't that classy," I said, sarcasm dripping.

He laughed as if I'd just let him in on a private joke. "I bet class is the last thing you want when it comes to making you scream. Am I right?" He took a step into my personal space, and just as I was about to zap him with a fiery bolt of magic, I felt someone else's familiar sexual energy brush against my skin.

Vaughn—my tall, dark, and gorgeous incubus.

He was here. Right behind me. I spun and gaped at him. "What are you doing here?"

"You might want to take a step back, brother." Vaughn glared at the idiot who'd been ogling me.

"Fuck off, asshole. My ten minutes aren't up." Frat dude's eyes were narrowed, full of anger.

Vaughn stepped in front of me, his neck and shoulders stiff with tension. My fingers twitched to soothe them as I held back a chuckle. I was more than capable of defending myself, and Vaughn well knew it. But this he-man display was seriously turning me on.

"Go," Vaughn said. "Before I bodily remove you from her presence."

Frat boy seemed to grow an inch taller as he stood up

straight, his muscles rippling with barely suppressed frustration. I was pretty sure he was half a second from throwing a punch, but one of his buddies came up from behind him and wrapped an arm around his shoulders.

"Hey, Zen. What're you doing talking to that pretty boy when the ladies are swarming?" His speech was slurred and it was clear he'd been drinking long before he'd arrived at the party.

"Zen?" I whispered into Vaughn's ear.

His shoulders shook with silent laughter.

Frat boy looked over Vaughn's shoulder at me. "I'll catch you later, sweet stuff."

I couldn't help it. The laughter bubbled out. I clasped my hand over my mouth and blinked back the tears of laughter.

"Bitch." Frat guy glared at me, but when Vaughn took a step forward, his buddy hauled him off across the room.

Vaughn stood his ground for a moment, watching the pair weave their way through the crowd, then he turned and raised one eyebrow as he stared down at me in exasperation.

I just grinned and shifted closer, sliding my hand inside his black sports jacket. "Why are you here?"

He leaned in and pressed his lips to mine. "To kiss my girlfriend." His tongue slid past my parted lips, and then he wrapped me in his arms and deepened the kiss, claiming me right there in the middle of the party.

My magic sparked to life, tingling everywhere as I pressed into him, my body heating up to explosive levels.

He tightened his grip around me, nearly crushing me to him in a delicious display of possession. "Jesus, Mati," he growled as his hand found the slit in my skirt. His fingers dug into my bare hip, barely maintaining control. "This dress should be illegal."

I pulled back and grabbed his hand. "This way." It was reckless and completely scandalous, but Janie and Chad were in the middle of the room, both engrossed in each other, and the only thing I could think about was touching Vaughn's bare skin. And that meant we needed a little bit of privacy.

"Mati?" Vaughn asked.

I tightened my hold around his fingers and led him to the back of the house to a darkened room full of books. It was a small library, most likely used by the resident advisor.

"Perfect."

Vaughn's eyes lit with understanding. And without saying a word, he lifted me up, spun me around, and claimed my lips in a punishing kiss as my back hit the closed door.

I wrapped my legs around him and lost myself to the magic pulsing through my veins.

He ground his hips into me, his hard shaft pressing against my center, and I let out a small moan of pleasure.

"It's been too long," he said into my neck and bit down on the sensitive flesh at my throat.

"Vaughn..." My body shuddered with need against him.

"Tell me you want me, Matisse." He pulled back, his eyes hot with lust. "Tell me it isn't just about the magic."

My breath came in short, needy gasps. "What?"

"Tell me I drive you insane, the same way I'm going out of my mind with the need to be inside you."

Slowly, I pushed his jacket off his shoulders, watching as it fell to the ground. Then, still pressed up against the door, I lifted his black T-shirt and trailed my fingers over his well-defined chest, leaving a trail of shimmering light behind. "You see this?"

He stared into my eyes. "Yes."

"This only happens when I lose control. Do I need you?

Yes. Do I need you inside me? God yes. And the sooner the better." I dropped my hands to the button of his jeans, stared him in the eye and said, "I want you. Now."

Vaughn's gaze dropped to my lips as we both stayed suspended in the moment, my words hanging between us. Then I popped the button on his jeans and his lips were on me, claiming me once again, feeding the hunger that possessed us both.

His mouth was everywhere. My lips, my jawline, my neck, my chest. And then his hand was gripping my hip, slowly working the strap of my G-string down. I was completely caught up in him.

Then magic concentrated at my wrist, grew hot, and pulled all the magic sparking between us straight to the charm.

"What—?"

My world turned black and all I saw was darkness.

CHAPTER 3

*N*oise and chatter filled my senses, followed by the slow fade of darkness to light. My feet hit the floor, and I stumbled backward a couple of steps, trying to regain my balance. I clutched Vaughn's arm—no, not Vaughn, a stranger—and let out a small gasp.

The guy chuckled. "First time to a mixer party?"

I blinked, my eyes finally focusing. I was back in the main ballroom surrounded by people and candlelight. "Uh, yeah. Is teleportation normal?"

"For the witch sorority? Yes. It's supposed to be the way everyone gets to know each other. But it looks like you might've been in the middle of something." He swept his gaze over me and smirked.

I sent him a flat stare as I straightened my dress. "Funny."

"I'm Rave, by the way," he said, holding his hand out.

"Sorry, Rave. I'm leaving." And without looking back, I drifted into the crowd, scanning for Janie. She'd been in the middle of the room the last time I'd seen her. But she wasn't now. Chad was there, glancing around, ignoring the coed desperately trying to get his attention.

"Chad!" I called.

He turned around, caught my eye, and moved toward me. The coed stepped in front of him, stopping him. He glanced up, clearly frustrated by the distraction.

"But it's a mixer, Chad. You're supposed to mingle with all the sisters," I heard her say with just the right mix of teasing and censure. "What am I going to put in my report?"

"Report?" I asked no one.

A girl next to me giggled. "At the next house meeting we're all expected to give a report of who we met. That one is the social chair. If she doesn't get names, there will be hell to pay."

Good gracious. Witches volunteered for this? I was willing to admit the magical decorations were cool and it was nice to socialize with people you didn't have to hide from, but this was taking things a bit too far.

Chad's gaze met mine. He widened his eyes and gave a tiny jerk of his head, practically begging me to come save him. Still not seeing Janie, I squared my shoulders and inserted myself between the coed and Chad.

"Excuse me, but can I borrow him for a sec?" I asked the girl who was going on about some term paper she just wrote.

"What? I mean, me and... ah... what was your name?" she asked him.

"It's Chad," I said. "And I really need to talk to him for a moment. I'll bring him right back." Clasping my hand over Chad's forearm, I dragged him toward the back of the house where it was a little quieter. "Have you seen Janie?"

"That's what I was going to ask you. She's not... I mean, this sort of thing makes her very uncomfortable."

"Yeah. I know." Shit. Where was she? "Okay, split up. We need to find her."

He frowned, scanning the room. "I'm sure she's—"

I'd stopped listening. Vaughn had just emerged from the back of the house, some tall black-haired girl clinging to him. A burning ball of jealousy formed in my chest, and I had to stop myself from snarling in her direction.

Jealousy was an emotion I just wasn't familiar with. It was ugly and clouded my senses. "Excuse me," I said to Chad and moved toward Vaughn, who was headed in my direction.

"Are you sure you don't want to go back to the office?" Skank-girl ran one fingertip down his arm. "It was so private there."

Vaughn grabbed her wrist and physically removed her finger from his arm. "Sorry. Taken."

My jealous monster fizzled out as I watched her eyes go wide with surprise. She'd probably never been so blatantly rejected before.

"What the hell happened?" Vaughn asked me when I stopped at his side.

I held up the bracelet. "Mixer magic. Every ten minutes we're supposed to meet someone new. By force, apparently."

He narrowed his eyes and then grabbed the bracelet and pulled, breaking it in one swift movement. The sparkling snowflake charms clattered to the floor. Leaning in, he pulled me to him and whispered, "My heart nearly stopped altogether when you disappeared like that... vanishing right before my eyes."

As an incubus demon hunter, he was used to walking between worlds. When people vanished it could literally be to another dimension.

"I wasn't a fan of it myself," I said. "And I'd like nothing better than to leave right this minute, but I need to find Janie. She was targeted by a few demons earlier this week and I need to make sure she's safe."

"Demons? But then why were we—"

"She was with Chad." I waved to her almost-boyfriend. "I had no idea the jewelry was spelled for teleportation."

He nodded and glanced around the room. "I don't see her."

"Me neither. Split up?"

"Sure. Text when we spot her?"

I nodded, gave him a quick kiss, and took off to let Chad in on the plan. Then I moved toward the grand staircase, which led to the second floor. A giant Christmas tree stood tall at the top. As I got closer, I realized every single ornament from the fluttering doves to the running reindeer to the flickering candles was animated with magic. It was an impressive display of witchcraft. And it called to me. I stopped mid-step, transfixed by the sheer power radiating off the tree. All thoughts flew from my head as I stared at the reindeer running in place. The spell was a perfect piece of magic. Without thinking, I reached for one, needing to touch it.

"Mati!" Vaughn called from behind me and grabbed my hand before I could snatch the reindeer. "It's a deflection spell. Don't touch it."

"What?" I was disoriented, had no idea what I was doing.

"The magic used on the tree. It's designed to keep anyone from going past it. Probably to keep people out of the rooms."

"Huh?" I said trying to digest what he'd said.

"Mati," he said again. "Snap out of it."

The fog cleared, and I shook myself as the magic tried to

grab hold of me again. Vaughn put his hand on my waist. His touch anchored me and everything stopped. The tree was suddenly mundane. None of the ornaments moved and it was just like any other overdecorated tree. "Whoa," I said. "Are you blocking its magic?"

He shook his head. "No. You are. I'm just lending you strength."

Damn. I was weaker than I thought. "Thanks. Let's go. Janie has to be here somewhere." It was clear I wasn't going to be able to search the second floor without him, considering the repelling tree, but if it was doing its job, it wouldn't take long to look around. I glanced over my shoulder at the party, scanning again before rounded the corner into the left wing. Neither Chad nor Janie were anywhere to be found. Dammit.

We did a quick check of the empty rooms, and just as we entered the right wing, I caught a glimpse of the red silk dress I'd loaned Janie disappearing around a corner.

"Come on," I said to Vaughn.

We ran, and as soon as we turned the corner, I stopped abruptly. Right there in front of us was Janie pressed against the wall, her legs wrapped around Chase, the other incubus demon hunter.

"Janie?" I said tentatively.

Chase had one hand up her skirt and the other one braced against the wall. Wave after wave of their sexual energy slammed into me, making me fidget with unease.

"Janie!" I called again, insistent this time.

She didn't acknowledge me at all.

"Should we go?" Vaughn asked quietly.

"No. This is all wrong. She has a thing for Chad. Not this... incubus."

Vaughn's eyebrow rose in curiosity. Then he scowled. "Shit. She's under his spell."

"Chase?" I asked.

When he didn't respond, Vaughn let out a heavy sigh and grabbed Chase by the bicep, prying him off Janie. "Dude. That's enough."

Chase let go of Janie unceremoniously, and without warning, he spun and sucker punched Vaughn in the gut.

"Oomph," Vaughn huffed out as he doubled over.

Chase stood over him, waiting for him to recover, ready for the ensuing fight.

I let out a loud gasp and clasped my hand over my mouth, horrified by what I saw.

Chase, the demon hunter, stood before me, his eyes glowing red... a sure sign he was possessed by a demon.

CHAPTER 4

"*J*anie! Move," I cried as I held both hands out in front of me, magic crackling from my fingertips. It was uncontrolled, raw power. It would likely only stun Chase and the demon, but if I hit Janie, she'd be toast.

"What are you doing here?" Janie stood up straight, her head held high. "You're intruding, Mati. Go. Now." Her tone was confident and commanding, not at all like the girl I'd helped get ready for the party.

Vaughn righted himself just in time for Chase to clock him with an uppercut. I watched in horror as his head snapped back and crashed into the plaster wall.

"Vaughn!" I cried as I launched myself at Chase, taking us both down. I landed on top of him, one hand grabbing his ear while the other had hold of one of his arms. My electric magic sparked and shot straight into him. Only instead of howling in pain as I anticipated, he let out a low groan and arched into my touch, reveling in my magic.

"Hmm," he said, wrapping his arms around me and

rolling until I was pinned underneath him. "You're not the innocent I was hoping for, but damned if you aren't delicious. A sex witch strumming with need. I could—"

Whack. The hilt of Vaughn's dagger bounced off Chase's head, knocking him sideways, but he didn't let go of me.

His eyes went wide with shock and then rage. Holding my arm with one hand, he leaped to his feet and swung me in front of him, using me as a shield. "You're going to pay for that, Paxton," he said to Vaughn.

"Let go of her, Chase, and we'll settle this once and for all."

I'd used all my magic trying to zap Chase unconscious, and now my legs were wobbly, barely holding me up. I needed to do something, anything, to fight back. Pure hatred and frustration bubbled up from deep in my gut. I wasn't a weak witch. Not when it came to magic or self-defense. This demon could go straight back to Hell before I let him get the better of me.

The demon laughed at Vaughn's words. "She's coming with me. So is the angel. The pair of them together." He hummed as if one of us was pleasuring him right there. "Naughty *and* nice for Christmas morning."

Oh, fuck that. My power might have been MIA, but my fist wasn't. No one got to talk about me that way. While the demon was gyrating against me, simulating his fantasy, I threw my head back, heard the satisfying crunch of his nose, and reached for his crotch, catching his balls in my hand and squeezing with everything I had.

Janie screamed and tackled me, while Chase howled obscenities and fell to his knees.

"Janie!" I grabbed her wrists, trying to keep her from

clawing my face. "You've been spelled. Chase is possessed by a demon."

Her wild eyes narrowed as she studied me. For a moment, I thought I'd gotten to her.

But then Chase said, "Janie, don't believe anything they say. You're mine and I'm yours."

His incubus magic filtered over us, making my skin crawl with a slimy demon taint.

Janie's gaze locked on his, and then she kneed me in the gut before scrambling to get out of my grasp. I stumbled after her while Vaughn yanked Chase up by the collar, and the pair went into full-on battle mode.

Janie stopped a few feet from them, clearly unsure of what to do next.

Vaughn and Chase were matching each other blow for blow, though I had a feeling Vaughn was holding back just a bit, knowing Chase was possessed and not an actual demon. But I also knew he'd do what he had to in order to take the demon down.

"Janie?" I tried again, holding my hand out to her. "Don't let the magic confuse you."

She glanced at me, her brows drawn together. She shook her head and appeared to study Vaughn and Chase, her eyes clouding with questions.

"Look inside yourself for your own strength. Trust your instincts. Would you really be up here with Chase when Chad is waiting for you downstairs?"

She glanced between me and the demon hunters battling a few feet away. Then, as if a veil lifted, her expression morphed to one of pure shock and horror. One hand came up and covered her open mouth as she shook her head in disbelief.

"It's okay. You were spelled." I took a step closer to her, knowing if Chase pushed out any more incubus magic, she'd be right back where she was before, under his demon spell. "Take my hand. It's all right. I promise."

She was too new to the world of incubi and demons, and as a trainee she wouldn't yet know how to deflect such powerful magic, but if we were connected, I could keep her grounded. Our fingers touched and her spine straightened as she stood tall and glared at Chase.

"You animal." Her voice was low and controlled. "How dare you manhandle me that way?" She tugged at the red dress, trying to pull the hem down to cover more of herself.

Chase paused for just a second, shooting her with a look of pure lust, obviously completely taken with her virginal persona.

Vaughn used the opportunity to kick him in the chest, sending him reeling back about ten feet.

I wrapped an arm around Janie and steered her toward the door. "I'm getting her out of here," I told Vaughn. "I'll be right back."

He was already hovering over Chase, zip ties in hand, ready to restrain the demon. The restraints were magical, so Chase would have to share his body with the demon for a little while longer until the Brotherhood—the demon hunters—could expel the demon and send him back into Hell.

Janie let out a little gasp, clutched her hand to her chest, and said, "No, not again."

And then her body faded and disappeared into thin air. "No! Janie!" Dammit. I'd forgotten all about the charms and the mixer spell.

I spun, finding Vaughn hovering over Chase. The other

incubus was passed out, his dark complexion pasty. "What happened?" I asked Vaughn.

"The demon fled at the same time Janie disappeared." He crouched next to Chase and glanced up at me with a worried expression. "Go after her. I have to get him back to the Brotherhood ASAP or he might not wake up."

The contents in my stomach churned with anxiousness. "Not wake up?"

"It's the effects of the possession. He needs the collective to regain his strength. There's no time to wait for them to assemble here." Vaughn grabbed Chase's upper body and hauled him over his shoulder. "I'll take him through the shadows and be right back. You need to hurry and find Janie. The demon isn't going to give up that easily."

I didn't even wait to see Vaughn slip into the shadow world—the world between ours and Hell, a place that made it possible to leave one point and reappear in another. He'd be back at the Brotherhood's mansion in seconds. And hopefully back to me soon after. But I had no time to wait for him.

Janie was vulnerable.

CHAPTER 5

I flew out of the room and down the hall toward
the magical Christmas tree. The ornaments were
animated again, and the desire to stop and admire the giant
Douglas fir was almost overwhelming.

The only saving grace was the panic swirling in my chest
for Janie. She didn't have the skills yet to ward off a demon,
and the thought of her soul being in danger made me
physically ill. I had to get to her.

Once I was on my way down the stairs, the sexual energy
in the massive room mixed with a small spark of my magic,
fortifying my strength enough to keep me going.

When this was over, Vaughn and I were going to have one
hell of a night in the bedroom.

At the bottom of the stairs I paused for just a moment,
scanning the crowd for my red dress.

There she was. With Chad by the refreshments. I let out a
small sigh of relief and took a step in her direction.

"Excuse me, young lady," a woman wearing a green velvet

dress, white gloves, and a snowflake diamond choker said. "Where's your snowflake charm?"

The impressive amount of magic radiating from the older woman nearly knocked me on my ass. There was no doubt she was the witch behind all the magic gracing the house.

"I didn't receive one." No need to tell her I broke it and left it in the middle of the dance floor.

She narrowed her eyes and grabbed my wrist. Tsking, she shook her head. "Don't try to play me, Ms. Ballintine." She snapped her fingers and the bracelet appeared in her hand. "Put it back on."

I shook my head. "I'm here on official angel council business, not to engage in your social club."

"I know why you're here." She waved a hand over the bracelet. The diamonds sparkled, then the silver piece of jewelry flew from her hand and wrapped around my wrist, magically putting itself back together. "It's imperative you appear to be following our guidelines for the safety of everyone. I can't have you looking conspicuous among my girls."

"But—"

She held up a hand. "I've neutralized the bracelet. Your sister and I met today, and we've come to an understanding about your future here at this university. See me after the party so we can discuss the details."

She strode off without waiting for my reply.

"Great," I muttered and took off toward Janie and Chad. Now what had Chessa signed me up for? Working for my angel-council-leader sister was turning into a grade-A pain in the ass.

"Janie?" I said, standing behind her.

"She's fine," Chad said, not looking at me. His voice was lower, scratchy as if he was coming down with a cold.

I frowned. "Chad?"

He glanced up, his eyes dark and irritated. "Janie's had a rough night. I'm taking her home."

What should've been protective came off as aggressive and overbearing. My alarm bells went off. Instead of challenging him right there in the middle of the party, I decided to go for a more subtle approach. "That's sweet of you. But she's staying at my place, so don't worry. She'll be fine." I placed a hand on her shoulder. "Janie, ready to go?"

She glanced over her shoulder at me, her eyes wide with fear. "Yes." The word was barely audible and with her rigid posture, I knew there was more to her reaction than what had happened upstairs.

"I said I'll take you," Chad said, his tone commanding as he grabbed her arm and yanked her toward the door. She stumbled and nearly fell on her face, but he kept her upright, practically dragging her toward the door.

"Whoa!" I called, running after them.

Chad nodded to the student manning the door as they disappeared outside.

A giggling freshman and her date stumbled into my path.

"Shit!" I veered but still managed to knock into the girl's arm, spilling the contents of her red Solo cup all over my silver dress. The strong stench of rum permeated my senses.

"Hey!" The girl spun, scowling with disgust. "Watch it."

I glared at her but kept moving. I didn't know what was going on with Chad, but there was no way I was letting Janie get into his car.

I burst through the front door and instantly shivered in

the cold air. "Janie!" I called, ignoring the wind chilling me to the bone.

"Mati!" I heard her call from the shadows of the large oak off to the right. "Over here."

I took off at a dead run. Within ten feet I spotted them.

And terror took over. A sliver of pale orange light shone from a partially opened portal right next to the tree. Chad was focused on the opening, chanting a spell I didn't recognize, while he kept an iron grip on Janie's wrist. She struggled, pulling and kicking, fruitlessly trying to escape his hold, but he was too strong.

Demon strong.

Dammit! The demon hadn't left. He was just jumping into anyone Janie was talking to in order to get to her. The only way to get rid of him was to take him into the shadow world and force him back into Hell myself.

I wasn't strong enough. I knew that. I hadn't recharged in weeks. But if I didn't try, Janie would be taken into Hell where she would be trapped, and as an angel she would fall, turn demon herself, and never even start living the life she was destined for. I couldn't let that happen.

"Chad!" I yelled as I threw myself between them, using my body weight to break their connection.

Janie collapsed on the lush lawn but immediately started scrambling backward.

Chad somehow managed to stay on his feet, but he loomed over me, his face contorted in rage. "You irritating bitch. If you weren't tainted, I'd take you instead."

Tainted? What the hell did that mean? "Looks like it's my lucky day then. Too bad I can't say the same for you."

He let out a sinister laugh and shot his hand out, grasping me by the throat.

Janie let out a cry of alarm behind me.

Magic curled and sparked in my palms, but as I clasped my hands around his arm, ready to unleash my worst, the magic fizzled out and left me empty.

Chad cocked his head to the side and then laughed. "This is who they sent to take me down? Pathetic."

Now that pissed me off. My magic was there. I could feel it stirring inside me, but for some reason it wouldn't surface. Were we in a dead zone? One cast by the witch council to keep witches in line? It was possible. We were on university property.

"Fuck off." I forced the words out despite his hand trying to crush my throat and then kicked with everything I had. My foot landed in the middle of his chest, knocking him backward and straight toward the open portal.

And taking me with him.

CHAPTER 6

The searing heat radiating from the portal told me we were headed straight to Hell. Panic seized my brain, and for a moment I did nothing. Just held on as we fell in what seemed like slow motion through the opening.

Then my fight reflex kicked in and I focused. In my mind, I pictured the demon hunters' large antebellum headquarters. The one place the demon would never choose to go. But as long as he was hanging on to me, I was in control of his destination. My magic might not be one hundred percent, but there was nothing wrong with my shadow-walking abilities.

As soon as we hit the portal, the heat vanished, replaced by a cool mist. The pair of us crashed into the shadows in a barren spot with no distinguishing surroundings. Just a grayness of nothing. I had no idea where we were.

My heart started hammering in my chest. I'd once before ended up in a desolate place where I'd been trapped, waiting for someone, anyone, to rescue me because my magic had failed me.

"Where the fuck are we?" Chad growled and jumped to his feet, already reaching for me.

But I was too quick. I darted to the left and circled around him. "Not in Hell."

He spun, his fists clenched in obvious frustration. Good. As long as he was focused on me, he wouldn't go back to find Janie. My magic started to bubble inside me the way it usually did when I'm shadow walking, and I almost grinned in relief. This was nothing like when I'd previously been in the void world. I was just in a deserted part of the shadows.

I could try to walk myself right back to the university, but if the demon had any skills at all, he'd just follow me. No. I really couldn't leave until I managed to expel the demon from Chad's body, send the demon back to where he belonged, and then I'd have to manage to get Chad back to our world.

But how could I separate the demon from the man? Magic? Not without hurting Chad. But that was better than letting the demon keep his body. Curling my hands into fists, I searched deep within myself for the magic spark, then I thought of Vaughn. I imagined the last time we'd been together. Let myself experience the memory of his touch, the tingles of magic that always formed once we connected. And then the way I felt when he loved me.

Magic strummed hot and bright from the depths of my inner being and strained to be released. "Hey, demon," I called.

His eyes glowed red with hatred. "Dirty witch."

"I might be dirty, but at least I'm not a stinking, soulless asshole who has to steal angels to get a date."

He snorted as if my insult was lame.

Maybe it was, but it amused me and that's all that mattered. "Get the eff out of Chad's body. Now."

"Or what?" He raised an eyebrow nonchalantly.

"Or this." I stretched out my hands and let a torrent of magic fly. Upon contact, Chad's body convulsed in place, unable to move or even fall to the ground. He was being kept upright by the electrical current of my magic.

After a moment, I cut the power stream off, not wanting to damage Chad too badly. I fully expected him to collapse to the ground, but the demon was too strong.

He glanced around wildly, then stopped and stood there, brow furrowed in concentration. Then he let out a roar. "Where *are* we?"

I shrugged, watching him closely. "Not sure."

He spun around and came right for me. His tall, six-foot frame towered over me as his red demon eyes bored into me.

This was it. Now or never. I'd either save Chad or... I didn't even want to think about the alternative. I braced myself, knowing if I ran it'd be useless. This guy was a jock, and even though I'd just tried to fry him, the demon possessing him was too full of his own kind of magic.

I couldn't compete with that. Not physically. I took a deep breath, tapped into my inner magic, and chanted, "*Seperatur. Seperatur. Seperatur.*"

My hands connected with the football star's shoulders right as he grabbed my hair and yanked. Pain shot down my spine as I contorted, trying to release the pressure. But he only pulled harder as he kneed me in the gut. Hard.

The air burst from my lungs, leaving me gasping. Everything hurt. My head, my neck, my back, my torso. But it would take more than that to bring me down. Instead of focusing on the pain, I concentrated on the nice boy I'd met earlier in the night. The one who'd been so protective of Janie. Who'd smiled down at her and taken her hand in his. The sweet guy she deserved.

Chad.

My magic pulsed under my skin, heating with intent. That's how witch magic worked. One feeds the magic with purpose. For most things, if a witch is strong enough, concentrates enough, she won't even need a spell or a potion. Though those things certainly made achieving the goal easier. Not this time. I was going to take him down by sheer will.

"*Seperatur,*" I said again, forcing as much power into the word as I could.

Red light appeared, coating Chad's skin as his eyes bulged. A howl ripped from his lungs and he swung, clocking me in the cheekbone, but I barely felt it through the magic coursing through me.

I was completely connected to Chad through the demon, and I knew without a doubt if I could hold on long enough, we could force the monster from him. All I had to do was keep a physical connection. But that was getting harder and harder by the second.

The demon within flailed wildly, limbs jerking and lashing out. Bam! Another punch. This one to my shoulder. I stumbled to the side, barely recovering before another one hit me in the kidney. I lurched forward, the blow nearly bringing me to my knees.

I wouldn't survive this much longer. My strength and my magic were waning. I had two choices: give one last-ditch effort to save Chad or leave.

Janie's lovesick eyes flashed in my mind, followed by the

awful knowledge that if Chad's body was taken to Hell, he'd never be saved. I'd already decided.

Getting my balance, I perched on the balls of my feet, dodged one more blow, and then lunged. My body hit Chad's full force, and we both went down in a heap of limbs. I plastered myself to him and unleashed all my magic, imagining Chad demon free and lying underneath me.

The demon cried out in agony and rolled, but I hung on, my fingernails digging into Chad's skin. The red light covering him grew until it surrounded both of us. And then with one last wretched cry, Chad went limp on top of me.

The shadow world went completely silent. My plan had worked. It must've. The light was gone and Chad's skin was clammy with sweat. His body was in shock, as was to be expected after a demon invasion.

But where was the demon? I placed both hands on Chad's chest and pushed him off.

And standing right above me in all his red-leather-skinned glory was the black-toothed demon, fire crawling up his arms.

CHAPTER 7

S *hit!*
 The flames grew and as the demon raised his arms, the fire shot straight at me.

I rolled to the left, barely avoiding getting singed. My heart hammered against my rib cage as I scrambled back on my feet, fully expecting another attack.

Except the demon turned to face Chad, his arms raised as he stared over his shoulder at me. "Take me out of here, or I'll burn him alive."

"What?" I asked, clutching my neck in fear. Chad, still unconscious, was helpless at the moment. "What do you mean 'take you out of here?'"

"You trapped me here, you bitch. Open a portal or something. I'm not staying here. Something about this place makes it too hard to think."

The flames died out and he grabbed his head, shaking it as if to clear the cobwebs.

I ran to Chad's side, prepared to shadow walk us both out

of there, but as soon as I dropped to his side a portal opened, and in came half a dozen demon hunters, Vaughn in the lead.

Fire engulfed the demon as he roared and ran head-on toward Vaughn.

I couldn't keep the cry from escaping my lips. But it was unnecessary. Vaughn was too quick with his dagger. It flew and landed in the chest of the demon.

Unfortunately, it did nothing to slow the fire demon down. Vaughn dodged and the next demon hunter launched his dagger. One after another, the hunters let their daggers fly, each of them landing in the torso of the demon.

Then, just as the last one met its target, the demon hunters formed a circle, closed in, and called, *"Finem!"*

The fire burned brighter and then winked out, leaving just a pile of daggers and ash.

"Whoa," I said softly.

"Mati!" Vaughn ran to my side and pulled me into his arms as the rest of the hunters disappeared back to wherever they had come from. "How did you get here?"

I leaned into him, resting my head on his solid chest, exhausted. "The demon jumped into Chad, and I was trying to bring him through the shadows to the Brotherhood, but we got stuck here. I don't even know where we are."

"You're in the shadows near our headquarters. Only the Brotherhood can step in and out of the shadows here. That's why you were blocked. But if a demon shows up, the area locks down and the alarm goes off."

I pulled back and grimaced. "An alarm? Took you long enough."

"What? The alarm went off right before we invaded. How long were you here?"

I shrugged. "Five, ten minutes?"

He frowned and his eyes clouded with concern. "You were here that entire time with a demon?"

I nodded. "He was possessing Chad, but yes. I had to force him out of Chad's body before I could shadow walk us back, but it sounds like we wouldn't have been able to go anyway." A ripple of fear shuddered through me. What if they'd never showed up? I'd be ash now instead of the demon.

Vaughn glanced at Chad. "He's awake now." Tucking my hand into his, he tugged me to Chad's side.

"Hey," I said, placing a shaking hand on his chest. "Are you all right?"

He blinked up at us. "Where am I?"

"The shadows. Do you remember what happened?"

He shook his head and pushed himself up, wincing. "Why do I feel like I've been put through a meat grinder?"

A pang of guilt slammed into me. "Sorry. You were possessed by a demon, and I had to fight you before I could force him out of your body."

"Holy shit."

"Yeah," I agreed.

Vaughn held a hand out to him and pulled him to his feet. But he didn't let go right away. He peered into Chad's eyes and then nodded once as if confirming something to himself.

"What?" I asked him.

"Nothing. Just making sure he's well enough to shadow walk."

I gave Vaughn the side-eye, but didn't question him further. All I wanted to do was get out of here and check on Janie.

"I'm good," Chad said, though he was swaying on his feet.

"Here." I wrapped an arm around his waist. "Just lean into me."

"Okay."

"Ready?"

He closed his eyes and swallowed. "Yeah."

I took a deep breath and then focused on the WΔM house. The shadow mist faded and a second later the dark of night surrounded us.

It took a moment for my eyes to adjust, and as we stood there, Chad clutching at me, trying to stay upright, but he lost the battle and slowly sank to the ground.

"Wow," he said to himself.

"You'll be fine in a few minutes," Vaughn said. He turned to me. "If you want to go in and get Janie, I'll wait with him."

"Thanks." I didn't hesitate. I couldn't leave without her, not after what just happened. There was no telling if more demons were after her angel soul.

The party was still in full swing with most everyone paired up on the dance floor. Looks like they'd found their dance partners. Everyone except Janie, that is. I spotted her sitting in a chair near the punch bowl.

I took a seat next to her. "Ready to go?"

"Yeah." She sounded so dejected, so lost, that my heart ached for her.

I reached over and squeezed her fingers. "What's wrong?"

She let out a huff of frustrated laughter. "What isn't? I made out with a demon, and the guy I like has vanished without even saying good-bye."

I jumped to my feet, unwilling to let her have a pity party. "Forget thinking you made out with a demon. He was possessing an incubus, and you were powerless to stop whatever went down there. And as for Chad, he's outside waiting for you."

Her eyes lit up at the mention of her friend. "Really?"

"Really. Let's go."

She jumped to her feet and we were halfway across the room when the witch in the green velvet dress cut me off. "I recall telling you we needed to talk."

Janie didn't stop. She was an angel on a mission. I didn't even bother to ask her to wait. Vaughn was outside. She'd be safe with him.

"I was busy battling a demon," I said.

She raised a curious eyebrow. "Can I assume he's been eliminated?"

I gritted my teeth. "Yes. You may."

"Good. Now, I've spoken to your sister. This isn't the first time we've had trouble with the underworld. And it's getting worse. Since the demon portal was blown open a few months ago, we've had three campus attacks. All of them targeted our less experienced witches. And now Janie. Your sister and I both decided it's best for everyone involved if the angel council keeps a close eye not just on Janie but the university witches as well."

"Okay." A ball of anxiety formed in my gut. Chessa had a bad habit of forcing me into situations that weren't necessarily in my best interest. And this practically screamed *Run! Run now while you can!*

"She's decided you'll be her eyes and ears. And the best way to do that without putting you in immediate danger is for you to join WΔM. Otherwise if you appear to be investigating, you'll become an instant target. A schedule will be delivered to your residence by tomorrow afternoon. Participation in our events is mandatory."

"Wait, what? You want me to join the sorority?"

"Yes, Ms. Ballintine. You'll be inducted at the next meeting." She swept off into the crowd, leaving me gaping after her.

Goddammit, Chessa! Joining a sorority? I was going to kill her.

CHAPTER 8

I found Vaughn, Chad, and Janie standing by Vaughn's black SUV. Janie and Chad had their arms around each other, their heads bent close, whispering. Vaughn, who was leaning against the driver's side door, strode to meet me the instant he saw me coming.

"What's wrong?" he asked.

"You don't want to know."

His eyebrows rose. "I think I do."

I sighed. "I just got signed up to join the sorority."

His lips twitched.

"Don't even say a word. I'm not happy."

"Chessa's idea?"

I just nodded. Then I glanced at Chad and Janie. "How is he?"

Vaughn's dark gaze clouded as he frowned. "He'll be fine after a few days' rest."

"You're not telling me something about him. I can tell."

He shrugged. "He's got magical roots."

"Yeah, he'd have to in order to be invited to the sorority party. Is he a witch of some sort?"

"No." Vaughn leaned in and whispered, "Incubus. But he hasn't been called yet. That's why the demon was masked when he was sharing Chad's body."

"Oh, damn." I glanced back at Janie.

She was an angel, and even though they were both young and likely wouldn't end up together forever, the fact was Chad's calling would lead him to a sex witch at some point, which would awaken his inner incubus. It made me sad for Janie when that day came.

"It's something they'll figure out when the time comes."

"Yeah. I guess so." I crossed my arms and shivered in the night air. "How's Chase? And how did the demon get the better of him?"

Vaughn scowled. "He was intoxicated, rendering his senses impaired. He's fine, but he'll be disciplined. Maximus is not happy."

Maximus was the leader of the Brotherhood, and while he seemed like a sweet older man, he didn't mess around. And in this case, I wasn't upset about that. Because of his actions, Chase had put Janie's life in danger.

"Come on. I'll give you a ride home," Vaughn said, opening the car door.

I shook my head. "My car is here and I need to drop Janie off at her house."

"Meet me back at my place?" he asked hopefully.

I cupped one hand over his cheek and leaned in, kissing him softly. "Not even a rogue demon could keep me away."

His eyes twinkled. "Good. I'll be waiting."

~

A HALF HOUR LATER, I dropped Janie off at the small house she shared with a couple of other witch students. The house had been warded against sinister forces and had private security. It was just about the only place she was safe.

"Thank you, Mati," she said before hopping out of my car. "I can't even think about what would've happened if you hadn't been there."

"But I was, and so was Vaughn. That's all that matters." I smiled at her. "And you're welcome. We've all had to rely on others to help us out from time to time."

"But not like that." Her eyes were wide with belated horror. "Demons? That's not normal."

"Not everyday normal, but also not my first rodeo." I frowned at her. "But it is something you're going to need to come to terms with. I mean, as an angel it's going to be your job to save souls from those very beings."

"Yeah." Her tone was wary, but I couldn't blame her. Battling demons as a lifelong career sucked. Especially when she didn't have a choice in the matter.

"Try not to worry about it now. Once you're trained and have the tools in place, it won't be as scary." Right. Even I didn't believe me.

"Good night, Mati." She pushed the door open and climbed out.

"Night, Janie. You looked amazing tonight."

She gave me a halfhearted smile and then took off up the walk.

After she was safely inside, I steered the car in the direction of the Lakeview neighborhood. Within fifteen minutes I was knocking on Vaughn's door.

"Hey, gorgeous," he said as he opened the door and tugged me inside.

"Hey, yourself." I wrapped my arms around him and melted into his solid frame.

And without moving me from his entryway, my incubus folded me into his arms and stroked his fingers through my hair repeatedly while I filled up on his strength.

"I'm so sorry, Mati," he whispered.

I glanced up at him. "Why?"

"Because you were left alone with that demon, and I didn't get back to you soon enough." He tucked a lock of my long dark hair behind my ear. "But I'm so proud of you at the same time. You took the demon on and expelled him from Chad. Do you have any idea what kind of inner strength that takes? You amaze me."

My heart swelled with love, and instead of answering, I stood on my tiptoes and pressed a gentle kiss to his mouth.

His hands adjusted, landing on my hips, his fingers digging into my sides. That one movement lit a small spark of desire from my core, and I opened my mouth, welcoming his tongue as he deepened the kiss with just a hint of desperate need.

I responded instantly, my entire body coming alive under his touch. "Vaughn?"

His hand moved up my side, sending tingles of magic everywhere. "Yes?"

"Take me to bed."

He stared down at me, his eyes full of desire. "You're sure? You don't want to—"

"I'm sure." I pressed my lips to his once more, claiming them as mine. I wanted him. Needed him. And not just to fortify my magic, though that was a nice side effect. This was all about needing to feel close to him after the battle.

Needing to feel alive. Needing him to know how much I loved him.

His lips still pressed to mine, turned up into a small smile. "Glad to hear it." Then he swept me up in his arms and carried me down the hall to his bedroom. I already had his shirt unbuttoned by the time we got there. So when he lowered me to my feet, I wasted no time slipping it off his shoulders and letting it fall to the floor, followed by his black T-shirt.

His chest was glorious. All rippling ridges and toned muscles. I could've happily spent the rest of the night just touching him. Well, except for that raw ache that only intensified the longer I trailed my fingers over him.

I stepped back abruptly.

Vaughn just grinned, knowing what was coming next.

I raised one eyebrow and glanced at the fly of his jeans. "Take them off."

His eyes never left mine as he did as he was told. The jeans hit the floor and then he stood there in just his boxers waiting. "Your turn."

This was my favorite part. I ran one finger over the curves of my cleavage, keeping my eyes fixed on his as his pupils dilated with lust. Then, in slow motion, I lowered the zipper on my silver-sequined dress. "If you want it to come off, you'll need to do the rest."

Vaughn gently turned me around and then his fingers replaced mine on the zipper, continuing what I'd started. His breath was warm on my skin as he lowered his mouth and trailed kisses over my shoulder, pushing one strap down and then the other.

The dress fell in a heap at my feet, leaving me in only my G-string and my heels.

"No bra," he said.

I shook my head. "Not practical with my dress of choice."

"Fucking hot, Matisse. Very hot." His fingers hooked into the strap of my G-string, and a second later I was standing completely naked in front of him, my body on fire from his gentle touch.

I pointed to his boxers. "Off."

He smiled that cocky grin he likes to wear when we're together and pulled me to him, placing my hands on the waistband. "You do the honors."

"Gladly." Kissing him, I slowly tugged the fabric from his hips one inch at a time as I stroked my thumb over his velvet shaft until he let out a strangled groan.

"Mati," he breathed. His boxers fell silently to the floor.

"You feel better than ever," I said wrapping my hand around his base.

He pressed into my palm and bent his head to scrape his teeth along my pulse, exactly the way I loved.

"Oh, God," I said, throwing my head back.

I felt the rumble of laughter deep in his chest but didn't comment. My desire always amused him. But as I stroked my hand up and then down and up again, all the humor vanished, replaced by shortened breath.

He seemed frozen in place as I touched him. Then abruptly his hand wrapped around my wrist and he gently pulled me from him. "It's my turn," he said huskily.

I grinned, all too happy to give myself over to him.

He pointed to the bed. "Lie down."

I did as I was told.

"Spread your legs."

His words shot another spark of molten desire to my center.

"Touch yourself." His eyes were black with heat and need. It was almost more than I could take.

But once again I did as I was told and ran one finger along my slick heat.

"Oh, Mati. Damn, girl. You're so fucking sexy."

I slipped one finger inside myself and moaned.

"Mine." The word came out in almost a growl as Vaughn hovered over me. His teeth scraped over my right nipple, causing me to jerk and arch beneath him. Then he moved to my left breast and flicked his tongue over the sensitive tip, making me lose all control.

Both of my hands landed on his hips, and I yanked him down, opening fully to him. "I need you now, Vaughn. Need you inside me."

Then he was there, his hardness pressing into me, filling me, torturing me with his slow movements.

I let out a frustrated growl and pulled him closer. "Deeper," I commanded. "Now."

His hips thrust and he anchored himself inside me. We locked eyes for just a moment, and then we both started to move, magic pulsing all around us.

Every nerve was alive with passion and yearning, every stroke building power, and the delicious friction nearly drove me out of my mind.

Light danced over my skin and spread to him, a cocoon of magic surrounding us. But ever since I'd fallen in love with Vaughn, the power boost from our magic didn't matter to me like it used to. All I cared about was the man above me, the one who made me feel alive and powerful and sexy as hell.

He quickened his pace, and I matched him thrust for thrust, meeting him with my hips. Our breathing quickened and everything except the wave of passion consuming us ceased to exist.

"Vaughn." I nearly whimpered as the wave built higher and higher until finally my muscles clenched around him and our shared magic collided, mixing together. As I let out one last cry of pleasure, the power soared into me, fortifying that place deep inside that kept me strong and whole. The place reserved for only him.

He held on, riding out my wave with me, and just as I was coming down, he thrust one last time and let out a groan of his own. A small stream of magic flowed from me to him, just as it always did. If I was going to sleep with an incubus, I had to expect that I'd share some of my power.

Vaughn rolled over, taking me with him so I was lying on his chest. He kissed the top of my head and said, "I missed you."

I kissed his damp chest. "I missed you too."

After a few moments, Vaughn ran his fingers down my bare arm. "So. About this sorority."

I let out a small groan. "Yes?"

He chuckled. "I can't wait to see you at their Thursday teas."

Lifting up on my elbow, I glared down at him. "Thursday tea?"

Nodding, he winked. "It's a tradition. Dresses, hats, and gloves. You're going to look—"

"Ridiculous!"

"No." He pulled me back down and rolled until he was staring down at me. "Adorable. And the perfect cover for security detail."

I sighed. "That's really going to be my life from now on, isn't it?"

He nodded. "But it'll be worth it to keep the next angel safe."

"You might have a point."

"You know I do. And I also know you. Even if Chessa hadn't ordered this, you'd have been the first in line to do something about it. Admit it."

"Yeah, okay, sure. When it comes to demons, I have a bit of a grudge. But that doesn't mean I would've joined a magical sorority. You know I like to work alone."

He ran one finger down the bridge of my nose. "Look on the bright side. Think of all the friends you'll make."

"Or better yet, I can just think of all the demons I can send back to hell or turn to ash."

He laughed. "Whatever works for you, babe. I'll be here when you need me. In more ways than one."

Vaughn bent to kiss me, and once again, I was lost in his touch.

Demons and sororities could wait. Janie was safe for now and I had an incubus to tame.

He pulled back and rolled over, reaching for something in his nightstand. "I have something for you."

I pulled the sheet up to cover my breasts and turned sideways. "What?"

"Just a little Christmas present." He held out a burgundy velvet box.

"But Christmas isn't for another week," I protested. "You want this to be a surprise, don't you?"

He chuckled and sat up, facing me. His lips curved into that sexy little half smile. "Too late now."

Oh damn. I was doomed. Head over heels for this incubus. "Come here," I said, crooking a finger to indicate he should come closer.

He leaned down, brushing his lips over my cheek. "Yes?"

"I don't deserve you."

He winked. "Yeah, I already knew that."

I let out a huff of laughter. "Well, maybe I can try to bribe you. Check the third drawer." It was the one he'd given to me for sleepovers.

His eyes twinkled with amusement as he reached down and pulled out the box I'd so carefully wrapped. It was long and thin.

"A tie?" he asked.

I snorted. "Right." Holding the velvet box up, I nodded to it. "Open them both on three?"

"You got it."

I sat up cross-legged and counted. On three we both ripped into our packages, laughing. Our chuckles abruptly stopped, and I sucked in a breath, caught completely off guard. In my velvet box lay a silver necklace adorned with a miniature dagger that was an exact replica of Vaughn's demon-hunter dagger. I ran a gentle finger over it, delighted by the spark of magic radiating from the miniature blade. It was Vaughn's signature and so personal.

"It's a pendant that calls me if you need me," he said softly. "I'm connected with the magic it holds. You just wrap a hand around it and think of me and I'll hear you."

Happy tears filled my eyes. This wasn't something one handed over easily. This was intimate and invasive for him. And completely unselfish. "I love it," I said.

He ran a thumb over my cheekbone. "And I love you."

My body heated with pleasure and I couldn't help the stupid grin that claimed my face. "I love you, too. Now open your present."

Grinning back at me, he lifted the lid on the box and let

out a small gasp. "Where did you get this?" Inside was a handmade dagger, infused with my magic to help keep his own magic stable when we couldn't physically be together.

"I had it custom-made. Then I spelled it."

He held it up, admiring the intricate carving on the hilt. "It's amazing. Thank you."

I gently took the dagger from him, placed it on the nightstand, and then pushed him back onto the bed. "Merry Christmas, Vaughn."

"Merry Christmas, my sexy witch." He tugged me back down into the bed and went to work on making the night merry indeed.

Goddess, I was a lucky witch. And even though it appeared my days were going to take a turn for the annoying, I didn't care. I had Vaughn by my side and that's all I really needed. All I'd *ever* needed.

I didn't know what new challenges would come, but for tonight, all that existed was me and Vaughn and the magic strumming between us.

DEANNA'S BOOK LIST

Witches of Keating Hollow:
Soul of the Witch
Heart of the Witch
Spirit of the Witch
Dreams of the Witch
Courage of the Witch
Love of the Witch
Power of the Witch
Essence of the Witch
Muse of the Witch
Vision of the Witch
Waking of the Witch
Honor of the Witch
Promise of the Witch
Return of the Witch
Fortune of the Witch

Witches of Befana Bay:
The Witch's Silver Lining

Witches of Christmas Grove:
A Witch For Mr. Holiday
A Witch For Mr. Christmas
A Witch For Mr. Winter
A Witch For Mr. Mistletoe
A Witch For Mr. Frost

Premonition Pointe Novels:
Witching For Grace
Witching For Hope
Witching For Joy
Witching For Clarity
Witching For Moxie
Witching For Kismet

Miss Matched Midlife Dating Agency:
Star-crossed Witch
Honor-bound Witch
Outmatched Witch
Moonstruck Witch

Jade Calhoun Novels:
Haunted on Bourbon Street
Witches of Bourbon Street
Demons of Bourbon Street
Angels of Bourbon Street
Shadows of Bourbon Street
Incubus of Bourbon Street
Bewitched on Bourbon Street
Hexed on Bourbon Street
Dragons of Bourbon Street

Pyper Rayne Novels:
Spirits, Stilettos, and a Silver Bustier
Spirits, Rock Stars, and a Midnight Chocolate Bar
Spirits, Beignets, and a Bayou Biker Gang
Spirits, Diamonds, and a Drive-thru Daiquiri Stand
Spirits, Spells, and Wedding Bells

Ida May Chronicles:
Witched To Death
Witch, Please
Stop Your Witchin'

Crescent City Fae Novels:
Influential Magic
Irresistible Magic
Intoxicating Magic

Last Witch Standing:
Bewitched by Moonlight
Soulless at Sunset
Bloodlust By Midnight
Bitten At Daybreak

Witch Island Brides:
The Wolf's New Year Bride
The Vampire's Last Dance
The Warlock's Enchanted Kiss
The Shifter's First Bite

Destiny Novels:
Defining Destiny
Accepting Fate

Wolves of the Rising Sun:
Jace

Aiden

Luc

Craved

Silas

Darien

Wren

Black Bear Outlaws:
Cyrus

Chase

Cole

Bayou Springs Alien Mail Order Brides:
Zeke

Gunn

Echo

ABOUT THE AUTHOR

New York Times and USA Today bestselling author, Deanna Chase, is a native Californian, transplanted to the slower paced lifestyle of southeastern Louisiana. When she isn't writing, she is often goofing off with her husband in New Orleans or playing with her two shih tzu dogs. For more information and updates on newest releases visit her website at deannachase.com.